"You need a man like me in your life."

Austin paused, gently rubbing his thumb back and forth across Caroline's lower lip. "And I'm going to prove it to you."

"What are you doing?" she asked breathlessly. As if she didn't know. As if she didn't want to touch him, to feel his rugged tight body against hers. As if she didn't want the heat of his desire.

"What I'm doing, darling, is prospecting. A man never knows when he'll hit an unexpectedly rich vein...."

"And you have?" she asked softly, a delicious anticipation filling her.

"You bet." Austin's voice was husky as his lips began to tease hers. "And I'm staking my claim...."

Suzanne Simmons Guntrum took a roundabout route, through various careers, to fiction writing. But, boy, has she arrived! *Christmas in April* is her eighteenth romance, and this Temptation has a special place in Suzanne's heart for two reasons: the Jeremy character is loosely based on her own son, and Christmas is Suzanne's favorite time of year. "The unequaled joy of watching my child unwrap his first Christmas present, and his squeal of delight" is the festive memory Suzanne would like to share with her readers.

She has also written under the pseudonyms Suzanne Simms and Suzanne Simmons.

Christmas in April

SUZANNE SIMMONS GUNTRUM

Harlequin Books

TORONTO • NEW YORK • LONDON
AMSTERDAM • PARIS • SYDNEY • HAMBURG
STOCKHOLM • ATHENS • TOKYO • MILAN

For Steven—heart of my heart.

Published December 1986

ISBN 0-373-25233-1

1

"JUST SIGN YER NAME HERE, miss," drawled the old wrangler as he pushed the stable register toward her with gnarled, leathery-brown fingers.

It had been a long time since anyone had called her "miss," Caroline thought, smiling to herself. She picked up the pen and signed her name in the dusty ledger. Then she straightened and looked the old man full in the face. "Do you need my home address in Denver, or will the address of my parents' condominium here in Keystone be enough?"

Rubbing his short, grizzled beard, the man shook his head. "Now that you mention it, I don't rightly know."

"Then I'll just give you both," said Caroline, quickly jotting the addresses down beside her signature.

The wrangler turned the stable register around and studied it for a minute. "Mrs. Car-o-line Douglas," he read aloud, dividing her given name into distinct syllables. He pushed the sweat-stained Stetson off his face and looked at her with what she assumed was a permanent sun-squinted gaze. "You ride much, Mrs. Douglas?"

She put her shoulders back. "I've done my fair share of riding, if that's what you're asking."

"That's what I'm askin'," he said, looking at her, his eyes not missing a trick.

Caroline met his skeptical gaze. She hadn't been on a horse in years, but surely riding a horse was like riding a bicycle: once you learned how, you never forgot. "Let me assure you, I'm an accomplished horsewoman." *Was* an accomplished horsewoman, she admitted to herself.

He tipped his hat to her. "I'm sure you are, ma'am, but it's my job to ask. Why don't we mosey on out to the corral and see what we can git for you to ride? 'Course you won't have much to pick from this early in the season. Most of the herd was moved south for the winter. Ain't been brung back yet."

Caroline nodded and followed him out behind the tack room and stables to the fenced-in corral. "We've certainly been having beautiful weather, haven't we?" she said sociably.

The man grunted and pulled the brim of his Stetson back down over his eyes.

It was true, Caroline thought contentedly as she looked up at the trees and the blue mountains beyond. The weather was beautiful, especially for this early in April. She took a deep breath. The clear mountain breeze was delicious on her face, even when mixed with the unmistakable odor of horses and manure.

"Guess yer best bet would be Lady, there, or Major," the old man gritted through tobacco-stained teeth. He propped his arms on the top rung of the fence and pointed out two of the half dozen or so trail horses in the enclosure.

"Which one would you recommend?" Caroline stepped up beside him and leaned against the wooden railing.

"Depends on just how good a horsewoman you really are, ma'am. Lady's nice. A bit tame maybe. Major now, Major can be downright contrary." The man shook his head and wheezed, "Yup, Major sure has a mind of his own sometimes."

Caroline studied the docile, doe-eyed mare and the big bay gelding in turn, then said on impulse, "I'll take Major."

The old man turned his head and spit into the mud-trampled straw at his feet. "Whatever you say, Mrs. Douglas. Long as you understand you ride at yer own risk."

"I understand," she assured him.

"I'll go git Major rounded up for you, then." He opened the gate and ambled into the corral. "I'd appreciate it if you'd close up after me, ma'am," he said as he swung his tough, lean body into the saddle of a mare tied to one side of the corral.

The man rode as though he'd been born and raised in the saddle, Caroline thought as she watched him maneuver the trail horse into position. That undoubtedly explained his peculiar gait.

He worked quietly and efficiently as he slipped a lead rope through the ring on the big bay's halter and led him back to where she was waiting. Caroline swung the gate open, and he rode through with Major behind him. She closed the gate while he dismounted and secured the lead rope to a post. Then the wrangler disappeared into the tack room. He reappeared several minutes later carrying a blanket, a saddle and a bridle. Major was saddled and ready to ride within minutes.

"Feel like I ought to warn you, Mrs. Douglas. These horses been acting mighty peculiar this morning. Real restless like. Something's botherin' 'em." He put his head back and gazed up at the sky and then at the mountains. "You never can tell about the weather this time of year, ya know."

"Yes, I know," Caroline agreed politely. She was no expert on the subject, but she knew it was the mountains that made Colorado's weather so unpredictable. They caused eddies in the main air currents, eddies that contributed to the sudden changes in the weather.

"You must have seen the chinook wind come out of the west in winter. It can melt a foot of snow in no time," the old man told her. "The Blackfeet called chinook 'snow eater,' and they knew what they was talking about. Just the same, I seen more than one dilly of a snowstorm blow up on a pretty spring day like this."

"I'm sure you have," Caroline said, looking up at the blue sky with its white puffy clouds floating here and there among the mountain peaks. It all looked perfectly innocent to her. Maybe the old wrangler needed eyeglasses. He looked to be seventy if he was a day.

Nevertheless, he gave her a firm hand up. Once she was settled comfortably in the saddle and the stirrups had been adjusted to the length of her legs, he squinted up at her and asked, "How long you plan on bein' gone, Mrs. Douglas?"

"I'm not certain," she murmured, putting her head back and basking for a moment in the unexpected warmth of the sun. Then she bent over and gave Major a pat on his sleek reddish-brown neck, talking to him all the while in a soothing, relaxed tone. The old man untied the reins and handed them up to her. She gave him her best smile. "Thank you."

He took in the blue jeans and the blazer she was wearing. "You dressed warm enough?"

"Yes. In fact, I'm too warm right now." She could detect a trickle of perspiration running down her back between her shoulder blades. She was wearing more than the man realized. There were navy-blue tights and a pair of thick cotton socks under her faded Levi's, as well as a long-sleeved shirt beneath her pullover sweater. In addition to leather riding boots that reached to her knees, she had put an old wool blazer on over the outfit. A pair of calfskin gloves covered her hands. She wore them more for protection than actual warmth. A wool scarf was looped casually around her neck.

"If I was you, Mrs. Douglas, I'd ride due east and take the first trail up the side of that there mountain," the wrangler advised her as Major began to move restlessly beneath her weight.

"Thanks. I think I'll do that," said Caroline as she grasped the reins in her right hand, dug in her heels and urged the bay to take this taste of freedom. "Don't look for me until you see the whites of my eyes!" she called back over her shoulder as she and Major took off across the grasslands toward the blue mountains beyond.

The old wrangler stood watching her until she rode out of sight. "Durn fool woman!" he muttered under his breath as he turned back toward the stables.

"WHOA! WHOA, BOY! Whoa, Major!" Caroline pulled on the reins and brought the big bay to a halt. She leaned back in the saddle and took a long, deep breath of fresh air. A clean wind with a heady fragrance of pine was blowing. The sun filtered down through the surrounding trees, highlighting a few hardy wildflowers growing here and there along the path.

Lord, it was a glorious sight, she thought, looking out over the mountain. It was immediately apparent, however, that she'd ridden farther than she'd first thought. She had a clear view across into the far valley. The stable and condominiums at Keystone were nowhere in sight. All she could see were mountains, a long line of trees and the glint of sunlight on the surface of a silver river far below.

Some distance away she glimpsed what was called "the prairie tree" in Colorado, the lowland cottonwood. Clumps of it lined the river valley on either side. Slightly higher up a series of timber belts began: dry junipers and piñon pines in the foothills; forests thick with yellow, or ponderosa, pine; and the tall, thin trunk and olive-green branches of the lodgepole pine. Higher still, on the northern slopes where there was more moisture, the pines were replaced by the soft green Douglas fir. And above these were the blue spruce and majestic Engelmann spruce, as well as groves of white-barked aspen, their branches still bare from winter.

But spring was in the air, Caroline mused. She could feel it. She could smell it. She could almost taste it.

"C'mon, Major, let's ride just a little farther," she urged, nudging him with the heel of her leather boot.

They took off along the trail, enjoying the brisk wind racing past them, each anticipating the rare union of horse and rider moving as one, thinking as one, savoring the precious moments of freedom they gave each other. As the trail widened into a high mountain meadow, they picked up speed. Major broke into a full gallop, his hooves pounding the spring grass.

Then out of the corner of her eye, Caroline glimpsed something white and brown; an instant later it streaked across the path in front of them. Without warning, Major let out a startled snort. He reared up on his hind legs, pawed the air with flailing hooves and came down abruptly, stopping dead in his tracks. Caroline felt herself being hurled through the air. She hit the ground with a thud.

"Oh!"

It was the last sound she managed to utter before the wind was knocked out of her. She lay on the hard ground, struggling to fill her lungs with air, feeling as though every tooth in her head had been jarred loose, every bone and muscle in her body rearranged at random. She finally managed to untangle her long legs and sit up. It seemed that nothing was broken, thank God.

Caroline got to her feet and hobbled toward the big bay gelding, who was standing some twenty feet away from her. "It's all your fault," she complained. "All right, maybe it wasn't," she conceded as she wiped her

palms down the legs of her jeans. She brushed aside the
dirt and leaves and damp pine needles that clung to her
clothing. "But it wasn't my fault, either, you know," she
grumbled, rubbing her bruised hip. "What do you say
we blame it on the rabbit?"

Or whatever the small, furry, fleet-footed creature
had been that had engineered Caroline's quite literal
downfall. "Now, now, Major, stay calm," she reas-
sured the startled animal in a soft tone, perhaps trying
to reassure herself a little, as well.

But even as she took another step toward him, the
horse was backing away from her, ears pricked and
alert, nostrils slightly flared. Major shook his head and
snorted, pawing the ground. Caroline watched as the
reins began to slip, and her breath caught in her throat.
If she didn't regain control now, the horse would turn
tail and run, taking off for home without her.

"It's all right, Major." She approached the trail horse
with one hand stretched nonthreateningly in front of
her, wishing she'd slipped an extra lump of sugar into
her pocket that morning. "C'mon, boy. It's all right. I
promise."

But it seemed that Major was not about to be pla-
cated by a few soft-spoken words. There was still
something a little wild in his large, dark eyes and in his
taut stance. The old wrangler had warned her that the
bay had a mind of his own. As if to prove it, Major gave
one capricious flick of his tail, turned and took off at a
gallop back across the meadow.

Caroline raised her fist in the air and gestured after
the horse's retreating form. "Damn you, Major! They

say the pig is a whole lot smarter than the horse, and you've just proven it!"

With another insolent flick of his tail, the big bay continued on his way, racing along the trail until he disappeared from sight. Caroline slowly lowered her arm, but it was another moment or two before she realized Major had left her standing all alone on a mountain high in the Colorado Rockies.

She was thoroughly disgusted with the horse and herself. "Now what am I supposed to do?" It was going to be a long hike back to the stables, that was for sure. "Then the sooner you get started, the sooner you'll get back to civilization," she told herself.

She refused to think about how many miles the hike down the mountain really was or whether she could even walk that far. She was in reasonably good shape for a woman her age, but she was thirty-six years old, and she was suddenly very much aware of the miles that stretched before her. At least she'd had the sense to dress warmly, Caroline thought, trying to console herself.

She lifted her chin and turned down the trail that Major had raced along only minutes before. As she walked, the unexpected exercise felt good to her cramped muscles. Although she had too much common sense to think she would still feel this way after a mile or two of hiking over rough terrain, she was almost enjoying the walk right now.

She forged ahead but quickly realized that this hike was going to be a lot tougher than she had first thought. Distances were deceptive in the mountains. The very clarity of the air was confounding. It was a common mistake for hikers to underestimate distances—common, often unpleasant and sometimes tragic. A mountain that might appear to be a comfortable hour's hike away could just as well turn out to be fifty miles farther on. Caroline was beginning to wonder if she could make it back to the riding stables before dark. If she was honest with herself, she knew her chances of that diminished with every step she took.

"So much for your little bid for freedom," she muttered to herself.

Then, off to one side and to her right, she spied what appeared to be another trail winding down the mountainside. Maybe, just maybe, it was a shortcut. One thing was clear. She couldn't spend the night on this mountain. And that's exactly what was going to happen if she didn't start taking some risks—and soon.

For somewhere along the way, she had become increasingly aware that it was getting colder. Much colder. She could feel the icy sweat running from between her shoulder blades down to the small of her back. If she stopped moving, it would evaporate just as quickly as it had formed. She drew in a breath of cold air and took off down the second trail.

An hour later Caroline found herself deep in the woods, her muscles shaky, her head a little light from the altitude. An annoying stitch had developed in her left side just below her rib cage. Her legs felt more like rubber than muscle and bone. And she was tired. Dog tired. She found a large, smooth boulder and gratefully sank down on it. She closed her eyes and simply sat there.

Minutes later she opened them and looked up at the dark cobalt sky on the horizon, then down to the smudge of gray cloud that drifted between the trees. The delineation where sky met mountain was hazy in the sudden gloom of a wintery sky. Something light and cold and slightly moist touched her cheek.

"Oh, no!" Caroline groaned.

Snow. One moment it wasn't there, the next it was. It started to fall at an incredible rate. The very air was heavy, pregnant with the stuff. In a frenzied moment she felt the sting of crystals pelting her face.

It was as though she couldn't breathe, as though the blowing snow was suffocating her. She could feel the icy tendrils wrapping around her throat and forcing themselves between her lips, stealing away her warmth and her breath.

Caroline knew enough about frostbite and hypothermia to realize that she had to keep moving or she was lost. She was seized by a sense of urgency. Cold engulfed her. And fear. She wrapped her scarf around her head and drew the fringed ends across her nose and mouth. Struggling to her feet, she set off along the mountain path, floundering, managing as best she could, knowing the snowstorm might soon obliterate any trace of the path from right before her eyes.

She leaned into the wind to keep her footing as she chanted over and over to herself. *I am not going to freeze to death in these mountains. I am not going to starve to death. I am not going to go insane.*

Hearing a sound behind her, she whirled and peered into the white fury at her back. She could scarcely see.

The snow was acting like fog, obscuring her vision beyond a few feet.

"For crying out loud, Caroline, get a grip on yourself," she exclaimed with a shaky laugh. She turned back to the trail. "I tell you, there's nothing there."

She plowed ahead, staring down, concentrating on putting one foot in front of the other.

"Oooh—" A strange, startled sound rose in her throat. She stopped in her tracks. There was something off to one side of the path. She quickly looked around. She couldn't see anything else, but there, there in the snow were the fresh tracks of a cat!

Caroline felt herself stiffen. The small hairs on the back of her neck pricked her sensitive skin. Surely the prints were too small to belong to a mountain lion. Perhaps they were bobcat tracks. After all, the bobcat was little bigger than a large house cat.

A great gust of wind swept across the trail in front of her, hurling spumes of snow into the air. When she looked down, the fresh animal tracks had disappeared, erased in an instant. It was as if the tracks had never existed, as if the slate were wiped clean.

Maybe she was hallucinating, Caroline thought, thoroughly dismayed. Maybe she had imagined the whole thing. Wasn't mental confusion one of the first symptoms of hypothermia? She gave herself a good shake. She mustn't start imagining things now.

Then she suddenly stood stone still. Smoke? Was it smoke she smelled? She put her nose in the air and inhaled deeply. Yes, it was smoke; it was no hallucination. Surely where there was smoke, there was fire. And where there was fire, there was warmth and people and life.

Smoke! She had never smelled anything so wonderful in her whole life! She continued along the path she was forging until she saw it, there, nestled among the trees: a log cabin with smoke curling from its chimney.

Then, just at the edge of her peripheral vision, she saw something move. It was an animal, and it was between her and the log cabin, moving stealthily, silently, among the trees, crouched against a snowbank. It wasn't a large animal, but it was quick.

Was it the bobcat whose tracks she'd spotted earlier? There was something vaguely wrong with that assessment, but Caroline was too tired and too relieved to care at the moment. She considered trying to outrun it, whatever "it" was, but she still possessed some common sense, which told her how foolish running would be in her exhausted state.

She moved toward the log cabin, her feet feeling as if they were encased in cement. She saw the animal skirt the woods and knew that it planned to intercept her before she could reach safety. She was less than ten yards from the door of the cabin when she came face-to-face with the stalking creature.

It *was* a cat! Not a mountain lion or a bobcat but a large, powerful, tawny house cat. And it never took its eyes from her, not for an instant. She was the trespasser here. That much was abundantly clear.

She held out her hand in appeasement. Her voice was scarcely more than a whisper. "Nice kitty kitty."

The big tomcat fixed its inscrutable green eyes on her with a look that seemed to say, "Nice kitty kitty? You've got to be kidding."

With her hand held out in front of her, Caroline made her way toward the cabin. She was nearly there when the cat haughtily turned its back on her. It sauntered up to the cabin door and began an insistent growl.

Caroline gave an exhausted shrug and followed in its tracks. She was no more than a foot or two from the door when the toe of her boot struck a snow-covered rock half buried in the ground and she lost her footing. She found herself sprawled facedown in the cold snow.

It was the last straw.

She simply lay there, too tired to get up, too tired to move, too tired to care whether she lived or died. She heard the door of the cabin open and pried open her eyes. From her vantage point she could make out a pair of large army boots and an incredible length of corduroy pant leg.

Then she heard a voice like the thundering of Grieg's mountain king, a voice that resonated along her nerve endings, sending a shiver down the middle of her back. It was a voice that could surely bring the very mountains down around them in a wild avalanche.

"Well, well—" the voice became a sonorous purr "—look what the cat's dragged in."

2

CAROLINE GROANED AND TRIED to roll over onto her
back. She was shaking, and her teeth were chattering.
For an instant irrational fear stabbed at her, making her
wonder if the man might not turn and close the cabin
door in her face. With fingers numb from the cold, she
frantically tugged at the scarf muzzling her nose and
mouth until it slipped down around her chin. She took
in a shallow breath of frigid air and pushed herself up
on her elbows. "Please. I need your help. I—I'm f-
freezing."

The man grunted. When he spoke, his voice came out
brusque and deep, somewhere between a baritone and
a true bass. "Yes, I believe you are! Get inside, Jake."
The order was directed at the cat poised in the doorway. With a flick of his tail, Jake complied. Then the
man went down on his haunches beside her. "Do you
think anything's broken? I need to know before I try
moving you," he said, wiping the snow from his eyes.

"No, nothing's broken," Caroline assured him.

She felt two strong hands reach down under her,
grasping her around the rib cage. Then she was drawn
to her feet in one swift and seemingly effortless motion. The man carried her into the log cabin, kicking the
weathered door shut behind him with one heavily

booted foot. After settling her in a straight-backed chair in what was obviously the cabin's main room, he gazed down at her.

Caroline looked up at the man towering over her. From her perspective he seemed to be all legs, long legs, lean and muscular legs beneath tan corduroys. There was something quintessentially male about the way he stood staring down at her, legs braced slightly apart, thumbs hooked into the belt of his slacks, hands splayed across his lean hips.

She could make out the straight line of his mouth and the enigmatic expression on his face, but it was the eyes that caught and held her attention. It was the eyes that mesmerized her. Caroline realized they were undoubtedly the bluest she'd ever seen. They were as blue as the Colorado sky reflected in a high mountain lake on the first day of spring. They were as blue as a Rocky Mountain river meandering in the warmth of the noonday sun. Yes, the stranger's eyes were as clear a blue as those of her own sweet Jeremy.

Words froze on the tip of her tongue, and the pounding of her heart drowned out all other sounds as the man's gaze swept over her. "Look, we've got to find out if you're suffering from frostbite or hypothermia. Do you understand?"

"Yes, I understand," she answered anxiously.

Squatting in front of her, he reached out with one large hand and touched her face; his touch was surprisingly gentle. Caroline inhaled deeply. He smelled of damp corduroy, hickory smoke and warmth. Like the earliest stars in the night sky, drops of melting snow sparkled in his lush, dark hair. His brow was knitted in a slight frown. And she could have sworn his eyes were an even deeper shade of blue than before.

"You can be thankful you had the sense to keep your ears and nose covered," he told her. "But your hands and feet could still be in danger." He reached up to unwind the scarf from around her neck and remove her wool blazer and leather gloves. The clothing was tossed aside without a second thought.

"I'm getting your floor all wet," Caroline murmured as she stared down at the beautiful hardwood. Puddles were forming at their feet as the heat inside the cabin quickly turned the snow to slush.

"Doesn't matter," the man said succinctly. Then, holding her hands in his, he studied each in turn before placing them back on her lap. "I don't see any signs of frostbite," he announced before going on to her feet. He pulled her riding boots off and threw them to one side; her cotton socks followed until he was down to her tights. Caroline could feel his strong fingers manipulating and massaging her toes through the material.

The breath caught in her throat. She couldn't stop the exclamation of pain that slipped from her lips. "Ouch! That hurts!"

"You're just lucky it does hurt. If you couldn't feel anything, then you'd really have something to worry about," he said, shaking his dark head. "Your hands and feet are cold, all right, but I don't believe you're hypothermic. A much more telling sign, of course, would be a cold abdomen."

Caroline didn't understand. "A cold abdomen?"

Before she realized what he intended to do, the man had tugged at her sweater and the long-sleeved shirt underneath and was placing his hand on the smooth and surprisingly warm skin of her abdomen. Then he ran his palm up to her left breast and pressed it over the spot where her heart was. She could feel her pulse pounding at the base of her throat. Her heart was slamming against her chest. She tried to swallow and found that she couldn't. "W-what are you doing?"

"The heartbeat and rate of respiration slow down when the body temperature drops more than three or four degrees. I was trying to determine if your pulse and breathing are normal," he replied in a perfectly natural tone of voice as he withdrew his hand.

She began to relax. "Oh, I see."

"I'm not a doctor, but it appears there's nothing seriously wrong with you," he concluded, straightening up to an impressive height. "You're cold and tired, of course, but you were very lucky, considering." He gestured toward the snowstorm raging outside the cabin window. "What in the world were you doing out walking in this, anyway?"

"It wasn't like this when I started out, and I wasn't walking."

"I see." It was obvious he didn't. He rubbed his chin. "When did you decide to walk?"

At that, Caroline got to her feet, bracing herself against the straight-backed chair. The difference in their heights—the man had a good six inches on her—put her at enough of a disadvantage without her sitting down while they were talking. "I decided to walk when Major decided to run in the opposite direction." She watched as his face drew a blank. "My horse threw me and headed back to the stables on his own."

"Your horse threw you?" he echoed.

"Yes. I'll no doubt have the bruises to prove it in the morning," she muttered, rubbing her hipbone. "It was an accident. Something ran across the trail in front of us. A rabbit, I think. Anyway, Major got spooked, and the next thing I knew, I was flat on my back. I tried to calm him down, but he just took off and headed back toward Keystone without me." Caroline put a hand to her head. "I walked for an hour, perhaps two, before I decided to risk taking a shortcut down the mountain. I'm afraid that's when I got lost." She sighed, then confessed wearily, "I honestly believe if I hadn't stumbled onto your cabin when I did, I wouldn't have made it much farther."

The man was very still for a moment. "Look, I'm sorry. I know you've had a rough time of it. It's just that I've had one hell of a week myself." He paused to run a hand through the thick curls at the back of his neck. "Jake and I were planning to spend a nice quiet weekend alone in the mountains."

"Believe me, this wasn't how I'd planned to spend my weekend, either," Caroline countered. After all, it wasn't as if she'd deliberately set out to ruin his solitude. His and Jake's.

Caroline's rescuer rubbed his jaw and shrugged. "Well, it looks like we're stuck with each other, so we might as well make the best of it."

She looked up at him and reluctantly agreed, "I suppose we have no other choice."

"You don't seem to be suffering from exposure, but it wouldn't hurt to take a few precautions until we know for sure. The important thing now is for you to stay warm." He took a woven throw from the sofa behind him and handed it to her. "I think a hot drink would be in order." His blue eyes narrowed in thought. "All I have on hand is coffee."

"A cup of coffee sounds w-wonderful," Caroline stammered as she wrapped the small blanket around her. She suddenly felt as if a thousand tiny needles were pricking the surface of her skin.

"It might be a good idea if you got out of those wet things and into something dry first. Come on—" the man grasped her by the elbow "—let's see if we can find something of mine you can change into."

Caroline allowed him to support her weight as they made their way into the adjoining room. One glance told her it was his bedroom. The furnishings, consisting primarily of a king-size brass bed and a mammoth oak dresser, were as large and unpretentiously masculine as the man himself. And to her surprise, the furniture was of excellent quality.

This was no primitive log cabin, Caroline realized as she looked around her. Deceptive from the outside, inside it was all beautiful, natural-wood floors and walls, hooked rugs and knotty-pine trim, antique oval mirrors and Windsor chairs, oversize oak furniture and select pieces of brass.

She stood in the middle of the room, watching dumbly as he took a pair of light brown corduroys and a flannel shirt from the closet and a pair of warm woolen socks from a dresser drawer. She couldn't help but notice the articles of clothing were nearly identical to what he was wearing himself. The Bobbsey twins—Caroline nearly burst out with an irreverent laugh—that's what they were going to look like. The Bobbsey twins!

"I guess you'll need to roll the legs up a little," the man said, glancing from the long, shapely length of her legs to the corduroy pants and back again. He tossed the clothes onto the bed and disappeared into the connecting bathroom. He returned with several thick terry bath towels. "You better rub your hair dry, too." He thrust the towels into her arms. "I'll go put the coffee on while you change."

"All right. And thank you," she thought to call out to him at the last minute.

He turned to face her, his bulk filling the door frame. "You're welcome. By the way, what's your name? We might as well introduce ourselves if we're going to be snowed in together."

Caroline stood there with the towels clutched in her hands. "My name is Caroline Douglas. *Mrs.* Caroline Douglas," she said, enunciating each word.

"Hello, Mrs. Caroline Douglas," he drawled with disconcertingly easy charm. "I'm Austin Perry." Then he smiled at her. It was the first real smile she'd seen on his face, and the difference it made was astounding. He was a devilishly handsome man, all natural charm and

perfect, straight white teeth framed by an unabashedly
sensuous mouth. Yes, the smile made all the difference.

Stunned, she attempted to smile in return. "Thank
you, Mr. Perry, for taking me in and for lending me the
dry clothes."

"You're welcome." He turned and walked out of the
bedroom, pulling the door shut behind him.

Caroline stood there a moment longer, the bath
towels still clutched in her hands, listening to the howl-
ing of the wind and watching the drifting snow outside
the cabin window. Then she dropped the bath towels
on the bed and began to undress, her fingers still cold
and a little awkward as she fumbled with the zipper of
her wet jeans.

AUSTIN PERRY'S LARGE HANDS FUMBLED with the coffeepot as he took the lid off and laid it down on the
countertop. He was filling the ceramic pot with water
from the kitchen faucet when Jake trotted into the
room, announcing his arrival with a decidedly dis-
pleased snarl.

Austin turned halfway around and bestowed an un-
derstanding glance on the oversize house cat. "Don't
care much for women, do you, Jake? Not that I can say
I blame you," he said, shaking his head as he set the
coffeepot on a back burner and turned the dial to me-
dium-high.

Nope, he couldn't blame poor old Jake for not liking
women. Jake's previous owner had reputedly been a
"lady of the evening" who had dumped him off at the
local animal shelter in the dead of a cold winter's night,

at least according to Austin's longtime friend, a Keystone veterinarian. Austin almost believed the story was true, too. To this day, the fur along Jake's spine would stand on end whenever he got a whiff of heavily scented perfume.

We all carry scars, Austin reminded himself as he took two stoneware mugs from the cupboard and set them on the kitchen counter. He certainly had more than he cared to count. No doubt his unexpected guest had her fair share, as well. She'd made quite a point of informing him that she was *Mrs.* Caroline Douglas. She'd acted kind of touchy about it.

Of course, maybe a good-looking woman felt she had to put her cards on the table with a man right from the start. And Caroline Douglas was a good-looking woman, even though she'd turned up on his doorstep with her hair all tangled and plastered close to her head, her skin a little chapped and her clothes wet through. She had apparently had a pretty rough time of it. Yes, he thought with a wry smile, apparently all God's children had their scars.

Jake seemed to be in complete agreement as he let out another growl of displeasure.

Austin frowned down at his feline companion. "Well, what was I supposed to do? Leave her out in the snow to freeze to death? Trust me, Jake. Caroline Douglas will go away once this storm blows over. I wish I could say the same about the rest of our problems."

It had been a week of nothing but problems! Austin's expression hardened at the recollection. He hadn't been lying when he had told Caroline Douglas that much. Yesterday he had come closer to knocking some sense into his father's head than at any other time in his life.

Hell, Austin swore to himself. Lately trying to reason with his father and his uncle was like hitting his head against a brick wall! Five years ago, when he'd agreed to take over the presidency of the family's ailing mining company, he'd never dreamed that same family would turn out to be the fly in the ointment.

It wasn't that he wanted to hurt anyone, Austin reasoned, although he'd been accused of that no less than a dozen times in the past few weeks. He was running a company that was supposed to show a profit to its investors. A company, not some charitable organization. A lot of people depended on him for their livelihood. In the end the responsibility was his and his alone. He understood and accepted that. What he didn't need was his own family actively undermining his efforts to do the job he'd been hired to do.

He turned the burner under the coffeepot to low and took the sugar bowl from the cupboard and a carton of dairy creamer from the refrigerator. He set them on the counter beside the coffee mugs. Then he stood staring thoughtfully out the window above the kitchen sink, his hands digging deep into the pockets of his corduroys.

Yes, part of his job had been to close down mines that had been in operation since the boom days of the 1890s. And yes his father had been bitterly, perhaps even irrationally, opposed to such an action. But the future of mining in Colorado wasn't in silver, or in gold, for that matter. The future was in the non-precious metals: uranium, tungsten, vanadium and molybdenum.

Austin recognized that his father and his uncle, and their father and grandfather before them, had been part of a tradition, part of a kind of mystique about silver and gold. All a man had to do, even today, was walk through the old mining towns like Silver Plume and Georgetown, the latter once known as the Silver Queen of the Rockies, to feel some of the excitement that previous generations of miners must have known as young men prospecting on the promise of a fortune. The fever truly got into the blood of a man, and she never loosened her hold until death brought the consummate release. That's what Gus Perry and his brother, Charlie, believed.

Austin tried to appreciate how they felt. He tried to understand, but his uncle and his father were both in their seventies now, and they were making their decisions based on emotion rather than good sound business sense. As current president of the company, he couldn't afford to do the same.

In truth, Austin thought grimly, he'd been prepared for a few unpleasantries when he'd been forced to close gold and silver mines that had been in operation for nearly a century. What he *hadn't* expected was the rash of crank telephone calls that he had been getting off and on in the middle of the night for the past two weeks. Then yesterday he'd received another warning, this one in the form of a letter. He refused to be intimidated by the threatening words, but he sure didn't need another nuisance in his life. And that's how he viewed this latest warning—as a damned nuisance!

His fist came down on the kitchen counter. He was going to end up with high blood pressure to boot if he didn't do something about the situation, and soon. He swung around, his face suffused with color. And that was when he saw Caroline Douglas standing in the kitchen doorway watching him. Her eyes were big and dark, as dark as rain in the high mountains. He tried, but he found he couldn't look away from her.

"I'll just help myself to some paper towels, if I may, to wipe up the water in the other room." That was all she said as she slipped past him.

Austin stood there for half a minute after she'd disappeared into the next room. Then he quickly went after her. By the time he reached the living room, she had dropped to her knees and was mopping up the melted snow from the hardwood floor. He could see a red stain in the center of each cheek and a tear or two poised on the tips of her eyelashes.

He reached out and brought her to her feet. Taking her face in his hands, he looked down into her eyes. "It doesn't matter."

"It does matter!" she insisted, turning her head away as if embarrassed or perhaps angered because he'd witnessed her tears.

Something told Austin she wasn't talking about the wet floor anymore. He held her at arm's length for a moment as his gaze swept over her. In his shirt and corduroys, she looked just like a kid dressed up for Halloween. Her face was scrubbed clean, and her hair was curling in soft tendrils around her face. She must have found one of his hairbrushes in the bathroom and used it to work out the worst of the tangles.

There was something intensely intimate about the thought of Caroline Douglas using his personal things. He was surprised to discover that he liked the idea. He liked it very much, indeed.

"Believe me, the floor doesn't matter," he said in a gentle voice, finding that his fingers had somehow become ensnared in her shoulder-length hair. He couldn't help but notice that it was thick and lush and had a natural wave through it.

For the first time since he had given her shelter from the storm, he took a really good look at her. By most people's standards, he supposed Caroline Douglas was a tall woman. She was probably five foot eight or nine without her shoes, and quite slender. That much was apparent, even through the baggy shirt and corduroys. Her features were nonclassically beautiful. Her nose was straight and on the small side. Her mouth was full and generous. Her eyes were large and dark. They were a fascinating kaleidoscope of colors—green, brown and yellow. They seemed to change color even as he watched. Just as Caroline seemed to change under his scrutiny. One moment she was a girl, the next a mature woman. It was intriguing!

Yes, she was intriguing, all right, Austin acknowledged. And perhaps because of that she was just a little bit dangerous, too. It wasn't every day that a beautiful damsel in distress showed up on his doorstep.

"Is the coffee ready yet?" Caroline prompted as she stepped away from him.

It was only then that Austin Perry realized he was still holding a swath of her hair in his grasp. He looked down at the silky strands, grunted and reluctantly let her go.

3

"COFFEE?" AUSTIN SAID the word as if it were some foreign sound on his tongue.

"You told me you were going to make some while I changed my clothes," Caroline reminded him as she wiped her wet cheek with the back of her hand. It was silly to shed even one tear over the afternoon's events. What was done was done, and that's all there was to it. There was no sense in feeling sorry for herself. She was lucky to be alive and in one piece, more or less.

"Yes—" the man's voice vibrated with the word "—I did say I was going to make some coffee, didn't I? It should be ready, as a matter of fact. Why don't you come into the kitchen and have a cup while I fix us something to eat?"

Caroline looked at him hopefully. "You can cook?"

"I think that's putting it a bit optimistically. Let's just say I'm capable of reheating."

"Reheating?"

He nodded. "I stopped at my favorite delicatessen on the way up here from Denver this morning. They make great cream of broccoli soup and corn muffins to go."

"That sounds wonderful! I'm starved." As if on cue, a growl emanated from her stomach.

He bestowed a sympathetic look on her. "How long did you say you were out there wandering around the mountains?"

Caroline frowned. Wasn't it right after lunch that she'd left her parents' condominium for the stables? She shrugged and confessed, "I'm not sure. Most of the afternoon, anyway. If I'd had any idea I was going to get lost in a snowstorm, believe me, I would have fixed myself something more substantial for lunch than an apple."

"An apple? No wonder you're starved," Austin exclaimed as he turned and headed for the kitchen. "What I can't figure out is why we weren't given some kind of warning. This storm is packing quite a wallop."

Caroline tagged along behind him. "I had my car radio on during the drive up from Denver this morning. I didn't hear a word about a snowstorm. Maybe they didn't know anything about it." She paused for a moment, then added, "You know, it's odd, but the old wrangler down at the stables tried to warn me. He didn't like the way the horses were acting this morning. He said they seemed restless to him. Like something was bothering them."

"Maybe the horses heard the weather report we apparently missed," Austin speculated with a flash of white teeth. But suddenly he did an about-face and grasped her by the arms. She could feel the surge of energy flowing through him. "I know this is a fine time to ask, but was anyone else out there with you?" He gestured toward the storm that raged outside the log cabin.

"No, I was alone."

He seemed to breathe more easily. "Won't your—family be worried about you if you don't show up tonight?" he asked, his eyes meeting hers as he released her arms.

Caroline knew he'd almost said "husband" and had changed his mind at the last minute. He must have noticed that she wasn't wearing a wedding ring. "No, my family won't be worried about me." She stared off into space. "I suppose if the old man comes back and finds Major hanging around the other horses and my car still parked by the stables, he might wonder where in the dickens I've gone to. But then again, maybe not. You never know about people. I wish I hadn't left my handbag and the keys to my parents' condominium in the glove compartment, though." She looked around the kitchen. "I'd like to notify somebody of my whereabouts in case they find my car. I don't suppose you have a telephone."

"Nope, 'fraid not," he said. "Are you worried that your parents will wonder what's happened to you?"

Caroline sighed and unconsciously straightened her shoulders. "They won't know to wonder unless they try to telephone me for some reason. My mother and father were aware of my plans to spend the weekend up here, of course."

His blue eyes narrowed perceptibly. "Do you always inform your parents of your plans for the weekend?"

"No, I don't, only when my ten-year-old son happens to be spending his spring vacation with them in Florida."

Caroline could see the edges of the man's mouth twitch in his effort not to smile as he leaned back against the kitchen counter and folded his arms across his chest. Apparently, she'd provided him with some amusement. "I don't know about you, but all of a sudden I seem to have worked up quite an appetite. Why don't you sit down?" He motioned politely to one of the spindle-back chairs around the country pine table. "I'll get you that cup of coffee I promised before I put the soup on."

Caroline inhaled deeply and took a seat. The aroma of freshly brewed coffee filled the kitchen. She hadn't realized how shaky she was still feeling until her stomach did an odd little somersault.

"Cream or sugar?" Austin inquired.

"Neither one, thank you," she said, settling back in the chair. He poured a cup of steaming black coffee and set it down on the table in front of her. "Thank you," she murmured gratefully as she placed her hands on either side of the mug. She sat there for a moment, then allowed her eyes to close. She bent her head and took a deep breath. The air was warm and aromatic, the room cozy and comfortable.

She opened her eyes and sat contentedly sipping her coffee as she watched Austin Perry work. For a big man he was surprisingly graceful in his movements. He took a large carton from the refrigerator and emptied what appeared to be the broccoli soup into an oversize stainless-steel pot. He placed it on a low burner to reheat. The corn muffins were wrapped in foil and placed in a warm oven. He took two stoneware bowls and matching plates from the cupboard above his head and set them on the counter. Spoons and knives and a container of butter followed. Then he filled another mug with coffee, added a spoonful of sugar and a splash of cream and sat down opposite her.

He studied her over the rim of his cup. "Anybody ever call you Carol?"

"Nobody calls me Carol," she said dryly. "Anyone ever call you Aus?"

At that, he choked, spilling hot coffee down the front of his shirt. He yowled and sprang to his feet. "Damn it!" he muttered, standing with his long legs straddling the chair.

"Are you all right?" Caroline asked.

"Yes, I'm all right," he assured her, trying to hold the steaming flannel away from his body.

She watched as he fumbled with his shirt buttons, barely managing to keep herself from reaching out to undo them for him. "If you give me your shirt, I'll rinse it out and hang it in front of the fire with my things," she offered.

"Thanks," he said, stripping the flannel from his back and handing it over to her.

"The T-shirt, too," she insisted.

"I don't suppose this is the opportune moment to make a joke about giving you the shirt off my back," Austin said, peeling the T-shirt over his head in a single motion.

"You suppose right," Caroline informed him, her cheeks growing warm. It was silly to feel that she had to avoid looking at his bare chest. Even with its smooth, powerful muscles and riot of fine hair running down the center, it was just like any other man's bare chest.

It was even sillier to think about the heat of his body and the faint but distinct male scent that clung to the soft material clutched in her hands. Austin Perry was no different from any other man. He put his pants on one leg at a time, no doubt. And it wasn't as if the male physique held any mysteries for her. After all, she'd been married once, Caroline reminded herself. She'd feel more like her old self as soon as she had some hot food in her stomach. Her light-headedness could simply be the result of not having had enough lunch. That decided, she headed for the kitchen sink.

Austin laughed softly in the back of his throat, and then hoped that Caroline Douglas hadn't heard him. There was something very appealing about her. He'd felt that right from the start. She was one sexy lady, of course. Although he had to admit that on her his corduroy slacks looked more comical than sexy, especially from the rear. And she was mothering him. She was a fascinating combination.

"This could turn out to be a very interesting weekend," he ventured aloud.

His guest stopped and looked over her shoulder at him. "Don't you think we'll get out of here t-tomorrow?" Her voice cracked on the last word.

"Not unless this storm lets up. Even with a four-wheel drive Jeep like mine, the roads would be treacherous. I don't mind driving you down to Keystone. It's not that far. But I won't take unnecessary risks to do it," he said in a somber tone. "I know it's hard, Caroline, but we're going to have to sit tight and wait the storm out here."

She leaned against the kitchen counter, let her head drop to her chest and moaned, "Why did I think I had to come up here this weekend?" Then she looked up at him. "Are you absolutely certain we're stuck here?"

He nodded. "There's no sense in my lying to you. I can't promise you that we'll get out of here tomorrow because I don't know whether we will or not."

"But my parents and son are flying back on Sunday," she said, her voice a mere whisper.

"Not if Denver is snowed in and Stapleton is closed down. And there's a good possibility of both if this storm is very widespread." He saw the expression on her face, and suddenly he wanted nothing more than to protect her. Odd. Protecting a woman hadn't been a strong motivating force in his life. At least, not up until now. Yet something told him this woman needed protecting and comforting. But damned if he knew how to go about it. "Hey, look, there's no sense in worrying yourself sick about it," he urged, one hand absently rubbing his bare stomach.

"Sometimes worrying is what a mother does best," she said as she turned the water on and began to vigorously scrub the coffee stains from his flannel shirt. She squeezed out the excess water and went on to his T-shirt. Then she turned off the water and carried the damp shirts into the living room.

Austin was close on her heels. "We *might* be able to get out of here tomorrow. Of course, from the looks of it, we won't know for sure until morning," he felt obliged to add as he came to a stop in the middle of the room.

"I see," said Caroline, her face clouding over again as she gave his shirt a good shake and tried to smooth out a few of the wrinkles. She draped it over the back of a chair to dry.

Austin watched her for a moment, then went from window to window closing the shutters and drawing the curtains. Immediately there was a sense of intimacy in the cabin. "It's time I put a couple more logs on the fire," he observed as he paused in front of the natural stone hearth.

It was then that Caroline realized daylight had slipped away while she wasn't looking. It was evening—night, really—and she could hear the chilling howl of the wind as it whipped through the trees surrounding the secluded cabin. She watched as Austin threw two large logs on the flickering fire. Afterward he turned and looked straight at her.

Heaven help her, but his skin was as sleek as satin! He was bronzed by the firelight, as if he had spent hours working under a hot summer sun and the acquired deep golden color was only now beginning to fade long after summer's end. The patch of crisp hair on his chest, arrowing in a fine line to his abdomen, had been bleached by nature to shades of gold and brown. He was lean and tight and powerfully built, all muscle, no spare flesh anywhere. He was a magnificent specimen of what a man could be, of what a man should be.

It had been years since Caroline Davis Douglas had felt this strange, wondrous, half-sick anticipation in the pit of her stomach. But she felt it now. It was surely a lifetime ago that she'd last wanted to touch, to experience the sensations of a man's flesh beneath her hands, a man's hair between her fingertips, to instinctively want the heat and the fire of another's physical desire. But she felt it now!

His eyes were dark like the darkest night, and beckoning. He stood there as she did, neither of them daring to breathe. The world moved around them in excruciating slow motion. The air in the enclosed room was charged with something musky, something sensuous, something primitive.

Then the fire popped, breaking the spell. They exhaled in unison.

Austin was the first to speak. "I better go get a dry shirt on." His voice sounded like soft footsteps on a rough gravel path. He turned and made for the door and the bedroom beyond.

Caroline nodded and swallowed hard. "I'll go stir the soup."

With his hand on the doorknob, he stopped and looked back at her. "Why don't we eat in front of the fire? It'll be warmer." Something flickered for a moment in his eyes. "I thought we might have some wine with our dinner."

"Wine sounds wonderful," Caroline replied. She could use something to calm her nerves. Wine would do the job nicely. Not that she was ever one to overindulge. But surely one glass could do her no harm.

Five minutes later she watched as Austin Perry walked back into the kitchen wearing a clean, dry, navy-blue flannel shirt tucked into the trim waist of his tan corduroys. His wavy dark-brown hair looked like nature's hand had tousled it once or twice on the way from the bedroom. Caroline found her own hands were tempted to do the same. She tried not to stare at him, but she couldn't seem to help herself.

What was it about this man?

It was true he had a commanding physical presence, but she'd known other big men in her lifetime. The Rockies tended to breed big men, in her opinion, men who were larger than life, who were willing to fight or even die for the next rich vein of silver or gold.

She pictured him as one of that rare breed of adventurers who still dared to delve into the very bowels of the earth and bring forth its precious metals. Or to climb and conquer its highest mountain peaks. She was willing to bet he also knew how to survive without the trappings of so-called modern civilization. There were few *real* men left these days, but Austin Perry was one of them.

Good grief, Caroline groaned silently, there she went again! She should know better than to be spinning daydreams about men, about this man, about any man. There were no heroes left in the world. No knights in shining armor ready to do battle for a maiden's honor. Chivalry was dead. Hadn't she found that out long ago? Surely at this stage of the game she wasn't foolish enough to revert to adolescent dreams about the opposite sex!

Still, if she was honest with herself, she had to admit that this man had more pure, unadulterated sexuality in his little finger than most men had in their whole bodies.

"Soup's on!" Austin announced, interrupting her thoughts.

He ladled the thick, steaming liquid into the stone-ware bowls while Caroline plucked the warm muffins from the oven. They worked in companionable silence for several minutes; then she picked up the basket of muffins and the butter dish and followed him into the front room. He set the large tray, holding their soup and wineglasses and assorted silverware, on the coffee table in front of the fire and motioned for her to do the same with the muffins and butter.

"I think we have everything but the wine," he said, surveying the cozy arrangement. He disappeared into the kitchen and returned with a bottle of cool red wine and a corkscrew.

"That looks delicious," Caroline said as he removed the cork and poured each of them a glass.

For a moment the light from the fire was reflected in the deep, rich color of the Burgundy. It seemed to take on a life of its own. It was as though the wine, in its heart and in its very color, had somehow captured the elusive miracle of reddest rubies.

"To the Fates," Austin said, raising his glass to hers.

"To the Fates," she echoed.

He tasted the Burgundy and declared, "Not bad, not bad."

"It's wonderful." Caroline took a sip and then another. "My compliments to your deli," she added some time later. "This is the best broccoli soup I've ever tasted."

"I'm glad you're enjoying it," he said, watching her wolf down her food. "There's plenty of everything if you want seconds."

"Oh, I couldn't possibly manage seconds," she denied halfway through the large bowl of soup and her third corn muffin. "By the way, where's Jake?" she asked, looking around the firelit room.

Austin rubbed his chin. "You have to understand that Jake is another order of cat altogether. He doesn't like being watched when he's eating, so he extends the same courtesy to others."

Caroline laughed uninhibitedly, then clamped a hand over her mouth when the laugh came out louder than she'd intended. "What you really mean is that he's a big old tomcat who's used to prowling at night," she contradicted, her eyes shining brightly.

Austin shook his head and reached for the wine bottle. "No, that's not what I mean." He refilled their glasses and went on, "Jake only runs wild when we're up here in the mountains. Back in the city, he seems to know he should stay put in his own backyard. Not that I tell him what to do. Nobody tells Jake what to do."

"Just like some people I know," Caroline murmured, leaning forward to retrieve her wineglass.

He continued as though he hadn't heard a word she'd said. "Of course, Jake was neutered long before I met him. Not that there isn't a tougher tomcat anywhere, regardless of the fact. Like any mature male, he isn't hung up on the idea of reproduction being the proof of his manhood, so to speak." He sat back against the sofa cushions and held his glass up to the firelight. He stared long and hard into the wine's ruby-red heart before taking a drink. "Yup, come to think of it, I guess old Jake and I think a lot alike on the subject."

Caroline raised her eyebrows in a quizzical arch. She took a healthy swallow of her Burgundy before she asked, "Does that mean you've been neutered, too?"

"Hell, no!" Austin sputtered, slapping his wineglass down on the table. It was a miracle it didn't shatter into a thousand tiny pieces on impact. "No, I haven't been neutered, but I do believe a man doesn't—in fact, can't—prove his virility through the simple, biological and often happenstance act of begetting offspring."

"Begetting offspring?" Caroline repeated under her breath. What *was* the man talking about?

Austin nodded. "The idea is juvenile, not to mention downright primitive. Let's face it, Caroline, any animal can do the same. I don't have any children, and chances are that I won't. After all, I am thirty-eight years old, and I'm not married. And I'm certainly not in the market for some mindless young female by which to assure myself an heir, whatever my family's opinion may be on the subject."

"Your family thinks you should take up with a mindless young woman just to guarantee yourself an heir?" She was trying to follow the conversation, but it was rather confusing.

"Yes, and for crying out loud, Caroline, I want someone I can talk to at this stage of my life!" He gestured broadly with both hands. "I want someone who understands what it was like to grow up in the fifties and sixties." He lowered his voice. "Do you know that I was introduced to a girl at a party last weekend, and she told me she'd voted in exactly one election? One lousy election!" He emphasized the point by thrusting his index finger under her nose. "She was twenty years old. She was a baby. What does a man my age say to a twenty-year-old baby? What does anyone say to someone who thinks of the Beatles as history and has never heard of the jitterbug or Sky King?"

Darned if she knew. "I used to wonder what it would be like to be Penny and fly around in the Songbird." Caroline sighed nostalgically. "There's something else I've wondered about for years. Whatever happened to Gene Pitney? I mean, when was the last time you heard his name come up in polite conversation?"

"How would you know anything about Sky King or his niece, or Gene Pitney, for that matter?"

"Why wouldn't I? I'm not that much younger than you," she said frankly. "I don't mind telling you that I was thirty-six on my last birthday."

Austin seemed surprised. "You don't look it."

"Thank you—" she acknowledged the compliment with a gracious nod of her head "—but I believe I do. Who knows what thirty-six or thirty-eight is supposed to look like? Maybe this is it." Caroline made a sweeping gesture with her arm that encompassed both of them. "This is certainly the way it looks on me."

"Thirty-six looks good on you. Real good." Austin picked up his wineglass and took a drink before he said,

"I couldn't help but notice you aren't wearing a wedding ring. Are you divorced?"

"No, I'm a widow," she said, looking straight at him.

"Sorry," he said hesitantly, "I didn't mean to bring up a painful subject for you."

Caroline smiled. "That's okay. It was a long time ago."

His curiosity seemed to get the better of him. "Why is it that an attractive woman like yourself hasn't remarried, then?"

She paused before answering. Recently she'd read someplace that the less light there was in a room, the more relaxed and comfortable people were talking about themselves. In the soft, rosy glow from the fire, she found herself perfectly willing to answer his question. "I was only twenty-eight when my husband was killed. He was crossing the street. There was a pickup truck. They say he never knew what hit him. We'd been married four years when the accident happened. It took me a long time to get back on my feet. It would have taken a lot longer if I hadn't had Jeremy to take care of." She glanced up at him long enough to explain, "Jeremy is my son." Then she gazed into the heart of the fire. "Those first few months after the accident, I was a zombie. Oh, I took good care of Jeremy. In fact, I devoted myself to him. But after he was in bed at night, I would often sit and simply stare at the walls." Caroline drank the last of her wine in a single gulp.

"It must have been rough raising a kid by yourself." The words came from Austin almost involuntarily.

"It was. It still is, but thousands of women do it every day in this country. At least I had my mother and father there to help me." She realized on some level that she was rambling, but between the uninhibiting effect of the wine and Austin's obvious interest, she found she enjoyed talking to him.

He moved a little closer. "Please, go on."

"I wasn't interested in men for some time after Jim's death. And, believe me, not many men were interested in a young window with an active two-year-old. So I devoted myself to Jeremy, to making a home for the two of us and eventually to building a small business in my basement. The business did better than anyone expected, including me. I still have an office at home, but we moved out of my basement long ago." She turned and looked at him. "Have you ever heard of Christmas by Caroline?"

Austin frowned. "Christmas by Caroline?"

"Yes, it's a wholesale Christmas designs business: Victorian decorations; handmade, commissioned ornaments; antique cards and tree decorations. We're in all the better department stores."

His blue eyes widened slightly. "You're *that* Caroline?"

"Yes, I am." She was pleased he'd heard of her.

"I see your stuff all over the place during the holidays."

"You do now, but seven years ago it started out as a one-woman operation in my basement. Then I got lucky. I happened to be in the right place at the right time with the right product. I never dreamed in the beginning, of course, that there was going to be a wholesale revival of interest in the Victorian era."

"I'm a firm believer that there's an element of luck in any successful venture," Austin drawled as he stretched his long legs out in front of the fire.

"What kind of 'venture' are you into?"

"Mining," he answered succinctly.

Caroline studied his profile by the fire's light. A thought suddenly occurred to her. "Mining? As in the Perry Mining Company? Don't tell me you're *that* Perry."

"Guilty as charged," Austin confessed, turning his head and smiling at her. "I guess that makes us even."

"I guess it does," she said, smiling back at him.

"I gather you've been pretty successful with your business, Caroline." He took one last appreciative swallow of the vintage wine they'd had with their dinner.

"Yes, I have been."

"Then I can understand why you haven't remarried. It takes a lot of time and single-minded determination, energy and hard work to run a company successfully. I know, and I'm not a working mother." He set his wineglass down on the coffee table and rose to his feet. "Would you like anything else to eat?"

"No, I couldn't possibly eat another bite. Thank you, anyway," Caroline said, realizing that all the while they'd been talking, she'd managed to consume not only a large bowl of soup but four corn muffins besides.

Austin gathered up the dirty dishes and the empty wine bottle and loaded the lot onto the tray.

"Don't forget this." She held out her wineglass.

"I have a bottle of unusually fine California wine I thought we might try while we enjoy the fire."

"Why not?" She smiled and set her glass down again.

He returned a few minutes later with the second bottle of wine and poured each of them a glassful before sitting down beside her.

Strange, he didn't seem the least bit affected by the wine, while she was almost tipsy, Caroline mused, neatly tucking her legs beneath her. Perhaps it was her low tolerance for alcohol, combined with fatigue and the warm food in her stomach, that made her so content and so utterly complacent about curling up here in front of the fire.

"You know, you haven't *really* told me why you've never remarried," Austin pointed out, his arm stretched out along the back of the sofa behind her.

So, he'd noticed. Caroline had wondered if he would. "As you said yourself, part of the reason was a simple lack of time and energy. That and . . ." She allowed her voice to trail off, unsure of what to say next.

"And?"

"And..." How could she say it without sounding like a naive fool or a raving feminist? She was neither, after all. How could she tell him that she'd fought long and hard for her independence—what woman of her generation hadn't—and she wasn't about to give it up for just any man?

"Well?" he prompted, as if he were perfectly willing to sit there all night, waiting for her answer.

Caroline took a deep breath. "I haven't remarried because I haven't found a man who meets my requirements."

"Meets your requirements?"

"Yes." She exhaled.

Austin sat up a little straighter. "Tell me, what are these requirements of yours?"

She wasn't sure she wanted to tell him, but the words came out all the same. "I want a man who loves me. A man I can spend the rest of my life with. A man who will be my lover, my friend, my companion. I want a man who will be a good father to my son. I want a man who's as successful in his own right as I am in mine. I want a strong man. A gentle man. A good man. Dear Lord, I want so very much in a man!" Caroline hadn't realized just how much until she put it all into words.

"Perhaps you want too much," Austin suggested in a reasonable tone.

"Yes, perhaps I do," she admitted with a shrug. "Perhaps we all ask too much of ourselves, of our spouses, of marriage."

They both fell silent. Caroline found herself staring down at his socks. Somewhere along the way Austin had taken off those hideous army boots. Good! She studied him by the fire's light and the soft glow of a lamp burning low in the corner behind his right shoulder.

"Is Perry Mining the reason you never married?" she wondered aloud.

He didn't say anything right away, and when he did, she was surprised by his answer. "No, it's too easy to blame it on the job. There are plenty of reasons why I've never married: personal ambition, the desire to retain my independence, the illusion that I had all the time in the world to find just the right woman. Then I woke up one morning and discovered I was thirty-five years old and no closer to finding the 'right' woman than I'd ever been. I wasn't even sure what I was looking for in a woman anymore. I don't think most men do know." He paused and ran a hand through his lush, dark hair. "I don't believe the majority of men *think* about it at all. We let our glands do the thinking for us. Which is probably one reason the divorce rate is so high." He sighed and shook his head. "My father once said that the only way I'd get a wife to suit me was if I whittled one out of wood. Maybe he was right."

Caroline met his statement with a challenging lift of her chin. "Do you expect a woman to be perfect, then?"

"No, I don't expect perfection in a woman. But I do require a few old-fashioned virtues like fidelity, trust, commitment. I don't believe that's asking too much, do you?"

Caroline blinked. "No, I don't believe that's asking too much. Have you always had such high-minded, old-fashioned virtues in mind for the woman in your life? Or were you one of those young men who sowed his wild oats and then looked around for the kind of girl he wanted to marry and found they'd all been 'sown,' so to speak?"

"Why, my dear Caroline, you sound strangely suspicious of me," Austin said, moving closer. He tucked a tendril of soft brown hair behind her ear and leaned toward her. "Are you intimating that I spent my youth seducing or at least accepting favors from young women, only to turn around and expect to marry a woman as pure as the driven snow?" he asked, his voice deep and seductive. He gently encircled the curve of her ear with his fingertip. His touch made her skin tingle. She shivered, and he moved a fraction closer, staring down into her eyes. "Do you really think I would take advantage of a woman?"

"No," she finally said, breathless.

"I'm not so sure about that," he said softly in her ear. "I haven't thought about seducing a woman in a long time, but by the gods, Mrs. Douglas, you do tempt me!"

He tempted her, as well, Caroline realized. She instinctively moved closer to him. She could see the blue of his eyes that went on forever and the strong, sensuous curve to his mouth. She put her hand out and encountered the soft material of his shirt and the hard muscles of his chest. She hadn't meant to touch him, but she had. She didn't think he'd meant to kiss her, but he did. His mouth found hers, and suddenly there was a raw, electric charge racing between them, striking them both to the bone. Caroline wanted to cry out. She wasn't prepared for the first overwhelming, impassioned feeling that flooded her mind and body. She wanted him—desperately.

It had to be the wine, or the romantic setting, or the soft glow of the fire, or even the cozy, snowed-in cabin. It had to be! Yet when he kissed her, she came alive. More alive than she could ever remember being in her life.

She was drowning in him and in the way he made her feel. Her senses were filled with him, with the taste and touch and scent of him. Her mouth was filled with his breath and then the sweet thrust of his tongue, which quickly became hot and urgent when he caught the tip of hers between his teeth and nipped and teased. She could feel his lips moving over her face like a cooling breeze, a balm to her burning flesh, leaving a small, moist path wherever he touched her.

"You feel so right, taste so right." He muttered the hot words against her mouth.

"Austin—" From the back of her throat it came, half growl, half cry, question and answer, protest and plea. She counted the furious beats of his heart, heard the wild pounding of her own like a cacophony in her head. Kissing him made her feel a little faint, all the while that it stirred something deep within her.

He was devouring her with his lips and teeth and tongue. Her fingertips dug into his shoulders as he pulled her closer and closer to him in a heated frenzy. She thought to pull back. She meant to pull back. But something kept her there in his embrace.

"Caroline!" Austin heard his voice come out sounding strangely hoarse. He raised his head and stared down into her dark autumn eyes. This was insane. He wanted her, but it was insane. She was melting hotter and hotter in his hands. It was indefinably sweet to sense her response, but it was insane all the same. He was burning up, and she was turning to liquid fire with his kiss.

"Please..." Her plea came on a breathless rush of air.

Part of him wanted her as much, more, than he'd ever wanted any woman. And he hadn't even meant to kiss her. It shouldn't have been so dangerous just to kiss her. He certainly hadn't meant for it to go this far.

"No, we can't. We have to stop," he argued.

Her voice was an oddly disembodied whisper. "We can! I don't want to stop. It doesn't have to mean anything."

"But it would," Austin said in his softest tone. "You know it would, Caroline."

"No!" Yet her cry rang with some precognitive knowledge of defeat. "It wouldn't mean anything," she promised with wine-sweetened lips.

He stared down at the mouth softened by his kisses. He gazed long into her eyes. "Yes, it would mean something, and you know it as well as I do." She chose not to answer him. He wasn't surprised. He released her and slowly moved away. "This isn't the time or the place, not after what you've been through today." He sat on the edge of the sofa, staring blindly into the glowing embers of the fire. Then he looked down at his hands. Damn if they weren't shaking!

Caroline sat up beside him. She stared into the fire's dying heart before mumbling, "I hate it when a man is logical."

"Somebody's got to be."

"But I..." She shivered and wrapped her arms tightly around herself. "Sometimes I feel very alone."

"I know," he murmured, putting an arm around her shoulders. "I guess we all feel that way sometimes. We come into this world alone. We spend a lifetime creating relationships with other people, and then we begin to lose them one by one, until at the end we're all alone again."

"How sad that sounds. And how very lonely. Do you really believe that?" she said in a pensive, melancholy tone. "What about our parents, our children, our friends?"

"Our parents grow older and become more self-centered, more interested in themselves than in us. Our children grow up and leave home. Let's face it, most of us are lucky to find one—maybe two—good friends in a lifetime."

"Then what does that leave?" Caroline asked. "A man and a woman together? I don't have that. I haven't had that for years." Her eyes glistened.

"Neither have I," Austin said, his voice husky. "I've never been married. I have no children...." He stopped and shook his head. "In the end, all a man has is a good woman—if he's lucky."

"We've got to stop this—" Caroline sniffed as she reached for her glass "—or we'll both end up crying in our wine."

He nodded. And as if by some unspoken agreement, neither of them said anything for a long time. The logs popped and cracked every now and then and slowly turned into a glowing pile of ashes.

"It's getting late. You've got to be exhausted after the day you've been through. Why don't you go on to bed?" Austin said, motioning toward his bedroom door.

Something in his voice made Caroline turn and look at him, but she couldn't make out his expression in the dark. He seemed removed from her, somehow distant. "Where will you sleep?"

She heard him pat the sofa between them. "I'll bunk down here tonight."

"I couldn't let you do that. I couldn't take your bed and make you sleep out here on the sofa."

"Caroline—"

"You're too tall, and the sofa's too short. You'll spend a miserable night. I wouldn't be able to sleep knowing you were out here tossing and turning—"

"For the love of God, woman, if you say one more word, I promise you that we'll both end up in my bed and *neither* of us will get any sleep!" He suddenly realized he was shouting at her. He relented and lowered his voice. "Go to bed, Caroline. Just go to bed, please."

She got to her feet and began to gather up her dry clothes from in front of the fire. She gazed down at the coffee table. "Our dirty wineglasses . . ."

He gave her a quelling look.

She quickly made for the bedroom door and only turned to look back once she'd put a safe distance between them. She hesitated for a moment and then decided to have her say. Her voice came out low and husky. The words were slightly slurred, but they carried across the room to him all the same.

"Thank you, Austin Perry. It's nice to know chivalry isn't dead, after all."

Then she quietly, obediently, walked into his bedroom and closed the door softly behind her.

4

DURING THE NIGHT the wind howled outside the bedroom window like a pack of wolves baying at the moon. It was a lonely sound that drifted in and out of Caroline's dreams.

She awoke late the next morning to find that the world outside the log cabin was still bitterly cold, white and hostile. Driving winds whipped the snow around as if playing a deadly game of hide and seek. One glance told her that she and Austin wouldn't be going anywhere. Not today. Not in this weather.

"Swell. Just swell," she muttered to herself as she again closed the curtains at the bedroom window.

Caroline padded across the floor in her bare feet and took a peek at herself in the bathroom mirror. She'd looked worse, she supposed. Once she was cleaned up, she was certain she'd feel better, anyway. Austin wouldn't mind if she helped herself to a fresh washcloth and towel. After all, she'd already made use of his hairbrush on several occasions. She drew the line, however, at borrowing someone else's toothbrush. She'd just have to make do. It wouldn't be the first time, Caroline reminded herself as she turned on the cold water and squeezed an inch or two of toothpaste onto her index finger.

Now that they were dry, she dressed in her own clothes again—shirt, sweater and faded Levi's. She straightened the sheets and the down comforter on the bed and tidied up after herself. It was the least she could do after Austin had generously vacated his bedroom for her.

Humming, Caroline picked up the pair of corduroy pants she'd worn yesterday and smoothed out the wrinkles before hanging them over the back of a chair. Next she gave the flannel shirt Austin had loaned her a shake and was about to fold it neatly in half when she spotted a piece of paper on the floor near her feet. She wasn't sure if she'd knocked it off the dresser or if it had fallen out of the shirt pocket.

She had intended to retrieve it and put it back on the dresser when something made her hesitate. She picked up the piece of paper and turned it over in her hand. It appeared to be ordinary twenty-weight white bond folded in half and then in half again, but something had been pasted to it, and the glue had partially soaked through to the back.

Normally Caroline had too much respect for personal property and privacy to stick her nose in where it didn't belong, but something spurred her to satisfy her curiosity this time. She unfolded the sheet of paper and stared at it for a minute.

"How curious," she murmured under her breath. "How very curious."

It was like something out of an Agatha Christie novel she'd once read. The one in which the murderer sends anonymous letters threatening everyone in the village.

A poison-pen letter, that's what it was called! Plain block letters had been cut from a newspaper and pasted onto the sheet of white paper. Caroline read the message once, then twice, shaking her head all the while. The third time she read it out loud: "This is a warning. Don't close down the Lucky Lady, or you'll be sorry. Bad luck will befall you."

She turned the paper over. There were no names on it. No special markings. No indication of where it was from or who had sent it. But she had the strangest feeling that whoever or whatever was involved, the message had been intended for Austin Perry. It seemed someone was threatening him.

"Good Lord," Caroline breathed. Surely Austin had seen the note. Surely he knew about the threat.

When a knock came at the bedroom door several minutes later, she nearly jumped out of her skin.

"Caroline?"

"Yes," she called back, quickly refolding the sheet of paper and stuffing it into the pocket of her jeans.

"I thought I heard you up. Are you decent?" Austin inquired.

Caroline opened the bedroom door and found him leaning against the jamb, looking very much as he had last night except for the growth of dark beard on his chin and the slightly slept-in look to his clothes. She met those clear blue eyes for the first time in the full light of day. "Good m-morning," she stammered.

"It's more like good afternoon," he said, a smile breaking across his handsome face.

Caroline glanced down at her wristwatch. "Is it that late already?"

"It is, but I have to confess I've been awake for less than a half hour myself. There didn't seem to be any reason to get up at the crack of dawn," he said, looking over her shoulder. They could hear the wind pounding against the walls of the log cabin like a battering ram at the castle gates. "We won't be going anywhere as long as this keeps up."

"Do you think it's stopped snowing yet?"

"We won't know until the wind dies down some. It's blowing too hard to tell." Austin ran one large hand through the dark curls at his nape. "How did you sleep last night?"

"Fine," she replied, dropping her eyes to the row of buttons that ran down the front of his shirt. "How did you manage on the sofa?"

"I've spent the night in a lot worse places." His tone of voice was matter-of-fact. "Would you like a cup of coffee?"

"I'd love a cup of coffee!" she responded whole-heartedly as she followed him into the kitchen.

"Hungry?" he asked as he poured them each a cup.

Caroline shook her head.

"Are you sure? I'm going to fry up a couple of eggs and a slab of bacon for Jake and me, anyway," he explained, opening the refrigerator door.

"Then you might as well throw in an extra egg and another slice of bacon for me," she acquiesced. Then she took a deep breath and plunged ahead. "Austin, about last night."

He took a carton of eggs and a package of fresh bacon from the refrigerator and set them down on the kitchen counter before looking back over his shoulder at her. "What about last night?"

She could feel his eyes on her and her face growing warmer by the minute. It may have been her idea in the first place, but Caroline wasn't sure she wanted to be having this conversation. She took a sip of her coffee and tried to swallow the small, hard lump that had formed in her throat. "Well, we'd both had a little too much wine to drink. We were snowed in together in this cozy, secluded cabin. There was the soft, romantic glow of the firelight. Perhaps it was only natural that something happened...."

He turned fully around, his blue eyes leveled at her. "Is that what you're telling yourself? That something happened between us because of the wine or the romantic atmosphere?"

"Yes."

Austin shook his head. "I don't agree, and I'll tell you something else."

She was reluctant to ask, but in the end she did. "What?"

"Sooner or later our curiosity is going to get the better of us."

Caroline's heart leaped. Then, deciding that two could play his game, she came back with, "Wasn't it curiosity that killed the cat?"

"Yes, but it was satisfaction that brought him back," Austin pointed out with a wry smile. "Sooner or later we'll want to have the satisfaction of knowing for sure.

Was it only the wine or the secluded atmosphere or the romantic firelight—" a dangerous glint appeared in his eyes "—or is it still there between us in the cold, harsh light of day?"

"Is *what* still there between us?"

He paused significantly. "Passion. Desire. Sexual excitement. Pure old lust. Call it whatever you will, you can't deny that it was there between us last night."

Her face flushed a painful crimson. "I'm not denying anything, and I don't believe lust can be either old or pure. I would prefer to think of last night as an accident. An accident, I might add, that won't be repeated."

There was an odd little silence while he weighed the thought. "You're embarrassed by what happened between us, aren't you?"

At least she could be honest with him about that much. "Yes, I am."

"Why?" he asked, lifting one eyebrow.

"Why?" Caroline's eyes flew to his face. "Because I'm not a kid anymore. Austin, and neither are you. We're two mature adults who should have known better."

"We should have known better than what? Than to play with fire?"

"Yes," she said as calmly as she could.

"You're being too hard on yourself, Caroline. On both of us," he added as he took out a large frying pan and set it on the stove. "After all, we're only human."

Caroline watched him break a half-dozen eggs into the skillet and add an equal number of bacon strips before she went on. "Are you trying to tell me that 'to err is human'?"

"It's true, isn't it? Although I don't believe we made an error," he said emphatically.

"Well, we certainly got more than we'd bargained for," she shot back.

At that, he laughed out loud. "I'd say a whole lot more than we bargained for. It's enough to make a man wish it would never stop snowing."

"That isn't funny," she said, pushing a strand of chestnut-brown hair back off her face.

"I didn't say it to be funny," he told her as he put three plates on the table. "Mark my words, Caroline Douglas. Curiosity will get the better of us yet."

Caroline knew she had to change the subject before things got out of hand entirely. "Speaking of curiosity . . ." She dug in the pocket of her jeans and brought out the note. "I found this on the bedroom floor this morning. I believe it belongs to you."

Austin took it from her. He scowled when he saw what it was. "Oh, that thing."

"Yes, that thing."

He tossed it on the table. "I take it you've read it, then."

"Yes. I didn't mean to pry. It was there on the floor, and I picked it up and opened it before I realized it might be something personal."

He shrugged his broad shoulders. "It doesn't matter. It doesn't mean anything, anyway."

She wasn't so sure about that. "Are you saying it's a hoax?"

"More like a nuisance." He took a spatula and turned the eggs and half-crisp bacon over in the frying pan.

"What are you doing about it?"

"Ignoring it."

"Then why did you keep this?" she demanded, picking up the piece of paper and waving it in the air.

"I don't know," Austin admitted. He grabbed it out of her hand, wadded it into a ball and threw it in the wastepaper basket.

That may have been the end of it as far as he was concerned, but Caroline found her curiosity wasn't so easily dismissed. "Do you mind if I ask you a question?"

"I guess not. But can't it wait until we eat? Breakfast is ready." The announcement came as Austin divided the bacon and eggs into three equal portions and dished it out onto their plates. He set the first one in front of Caroline and the second at his own place. The third plate went on the floor of the storage room just off the kitchen for a seemingly ravenous Jake. Before Austin closed the door, Caroline glimpsed the cat attacking his food with a vengeance usually reserved for prey.

"Now what did you want to ask me?" Austin prompted halfway through their meal.

Caroline set her coffee cup down and looked at him across the kitchen table. "Who or what is the Lucky Lady?"

"That's easy. The Lucky Lady's a gold mine."

She thought about that for a good thirty seconds or more before saying, "A gold mine, I take it, that you're about to close down."

Austin polished off the bacon and eggs on his plate and took a drink of coffee. "We've been in the process of closing the Lucky Lady for the past several weeks."

"We?"

"The Perry Mining Company. Specifically, me as president."

"It would seem that someone doesn't like what you're doing," Caroline pointed out.

"The president of any company has to make unpopular decisions at times. It goes with the territory. You must know that from your own experience."

She nodded. "True, but I've never received an anonymous, threatening letter as a result of those decisions."

Austin sighed and pushed his plate away. "Unfortunately, in this case there's a lot of so-called sentiment attached to the closing of the operation. You see, the Lucky Lady was the first mine my great-grandfather staked a claim to when he migrated to Colorado in 1890."

"I see what you mean by unpopular," she said, convinced. "Do you know who in particular opposes closing the Lucky Lady?"

He stroked the stubble on his chin and took another swallow of hot coffee. "Almost half the board of directors, several old-timers who invested in the company back in the thirties, my Uncle Charlie and my own father," he said dryly.

"Your own father?" she repeated, her eyes opening wide.

"Yup. It's not just the Lucky Lady, either. It's the Silver Lady and a whole series of gold and silver mines that were pretty well played out years ago. It's too expensive to operate them with the price of precious metals what it is today. They're costing the company more than they're worth. We can't afford to keep them open for sentimental reasons."

"In other words," Caroline said glumly, "you're caught in the middle. Between a rock and a hard place, as my father is fond of saying."

Austin leaned back in his chair. "You can say that again," he echoed cynically. "There are times I wish I'd never agreed to take over the presidency when Gus decided to retire five years ago."

"Gus is your father?"

He nodded. "Gus Perry. Age: seventy-five. Disposition: cantankerous, meddlesome and a little foolish when it comes to pretty young girls." He sighed. "Things would have been different if my mother had lived. She was always the go-between, the mediator, the one to patch up any damage done by the rest of us in the heat of the moment. She always made peace between the warring parties. But my mother lost her battle against cancer just after I took over control of the company, and that has made all the difference." Austin shook his head sadly. "I feel sorry for my father, but he's making things real tough for himself and for me right now."

Caroline understood well enough. She only hoped her questions hadn't opened a Pandora's box. "If it's any comfort to you, I suppose we've all been through difficult times with our parents," she said philosophically. "Their expectations for us don't cease simply because we're adults. And once they're retired, it seems they have even more time on their hands to think of ways to get us to do what *they* think we should."

Austin broke into a brief smile. "You've been reading my mind again."

"Not really. It's just that I've had some experience with my own parents. My father retired several years ago." She took a fortifying breath. "I assume you've tried talking to your father."

"Yes—" his face took on an uncompromising look "—for all the good it's done. Lord knows, I love my father, Caroline, but we don't seem to talk anymore. Maybe we never did. Maybe we've only been kidding ourselves, covering up the fact that we don't really communicate, we only go through the motions. I can't get Gus to understand that I won't, that I can't, compromise my position this time because of his feelings." Slowly he shook his head. "My father doesn't understand because he doesn't *want* to understand. He refuses to listen to reason."

"Reason?"

"Yes, reason, as in good sound business sense. He refuses to acknowledge the economic truths about running a company that is no longer a privately held corporation, as it was in his day."

"Perhaps it's not that he refuses to see reason as you define it. Perhaps it's simply that money no longer has the same importance in your father's life as it once did,"

Caroline suggested carefully. "Couldn't you agree on some kind of compromise?"

"How? A mine is either in operation or it's shut down." He gave her a funny look. "No doubt you think I should keep it open as a tourist attraction or something."

She made an expressive face. "I suppose your father would hate that."

"Gus would blow up the Lucky Lady before he'd let that happen to her," he stated as if there wasn't the slightest doubt in his mind.

Caroline decided to leave the subject alone. "Then, as president of the Perry Mining Company, it looks like you'll have to do whatever it is you think you have to do," she concluded with a shrug.

"Exactly the conclusion I came to."

"What are you going to do about the poison-pen letter?" She felt she had to ask.

"Nothing. I think it's meaningless. Some disgruntled old codger probably sent it, trying to scare me off. I'm sure nothing more will come of it," Austin assured her.

"I suppose you're right," Caroline agreed, getting to her feet and starting to clear away their dirty breakfast dishes. "I'll wash up. It's the least I can do when you've done all the cooking."

He smiled at her. "In that case, I think I'll sit here and have another cup of coffee."

"Let me get it for you."

"Thank you," he said, suddenly looking very pleased with himself and very much like the king of the castle.

"By the way, do you happen to play gin rummy?" he asked a few minutes later once the dishes were washed and stacked in the drain rack to dry.

"Gin rummy? I play a little," she said hesitantly.

Austin took a deck of playing cards from a kitchen drawer and began to shuffle them like an expert. "Shall we say a penny a point?"

"You're on!"

"LET ME SEE," she murmured, chewing thoughtfully on the end of the pencil she held in her hand, "six plus seven are thirteen, carry the one..." She scribbled some numbers on the score pad in front of her. Then she looked up and flashed him a smile. She tried not to be too smug. "You owe me a grand total of thirty-seven dollars and fifty-three cents."

On the opposite side of the kitchen table, Austin stretched out his long arms and his even longer legs, stifling an errant yawn. "How long have we been at this card game?"

She looked at the clock on the kitchen wall. "Except for a short break every now and then and whatever time it took for us to grab some sandwiches and leftover soup, we've been playing gin rummy since one o'clock this afternoon. That's nearly eight hours."

He blinked with surprise. "And how much did you say I owe you?"

She smiled at him condescendingly. "Thirty-seven dollars and fifty-three cents."

He brooded for a moment, whistling between his teeth. "Why do I get the distinct feeling I've been had?" he inquired, not altogether seriously.

"Why, Mr. Perry, whatever do you mean?"

He speared her with that icy-blue stare of his. "What I mean, Mrs. Douglas, is that I rarely lose at cards, even gin rummy. And I've certainly never lost to a woman before."

She clicked her tongue disapprovingly. "Be careful, it's showing."

"What is?" he asked guardedly.

She left an eloquent pause. Then, "Your male chauvinism."

"My what?"

"Your male chauvinism, as in male chauvinist pig."

"My dear Caroline, I believe that expression went out of style back in the seventies," Austin said, grimly amused.

"So did male chauvinism," she said a shade haughtily. "Surely you aren't one of those men who thinks he can do anything better than a woman simply by virtue of being born a man, are you?" She decided to answer her own question. "No, of course not. You couldn't be."

"You're half right, anyway," Austin admitted with what sounded suspiciously like a chuckle.

"Half right?"

He grinned at her. "I've always thought being born a man was a definite virtue."

"You can't take any credit for an accident of birth," Caroline reminded him with a certain civility.

"But accidents do happen, don't they? Like the little accident that took place between the two of us last night." He was staring at her. It made Caroline nervous.

Catching the tip of her tongue between her teeth, she finally asked, "What are you staring at?"

After a moment he said, "Your mouth."

"Why?" She felt a little stunned.

"Because it's beautiful. Because I can't help wondering if it always tastes like sweet red wine. Because I can't stop thinking about the way it felt under mine—all soft and hot and deliciously moist."

Her heart began to pound. "Austin, please—"

"Please what? Please stop, Austin? Please go on, Austin? Please tell me more? Please kiss me again and satisfy the curiosity that's been eating away at both of us all afternoon and all evening?"

Her face reddened. "No!"

"Yes!" he charged.

"No, really," she said, struggling to keep her voice even.

A flicker of disbelief crossed his handsome face. "Then prove it," he said quietly.

Her breath caught audibly. "Prove it?"

His blue eyes narrowed. "Yes, prove it. Come over here and kiss me. I dare you to prove to both of us that I'm wrong."

Caroline accepted the dare, all the while knowing that a trap was closing around her. Damn the man, it seemed he had played his little game and won, this time. Caroline's voice was no more than a whisper as she conceded, "All right."

She got to her feet and came around to Austin's side of the kitchen table. Leaning toward him, her hands reaching out to touch his shoulders, she took a deep breath and brought her face down to his. Her eyes closed at the last moment when their lips touched. He got no more than a quick peck before she went to pull back.

His arms went around her like a vise, halting her retreat. "Surely you don't call that a kiss," he challenged as his mouth covered hers and he took her breath away.

The next thing Caroline knew, she was sitting on his lap with her arms wrapped around his neck. He had that effect on her. All her good intentions flew out the window the moment he kissed her, the moment he touched her.

With muffled groans Austin found her mouth again and again. His became hard and hungry as he took hers. His tongue was hotly persuasive as it slipped between her parted lips to taste her sweet, oh, so sweet, surrender. She wrapped herself more tightly around him, her fingers lost in the lush, thick curls at the back of his head.

"Kiss me. Touch me," came her hoarsely whispered plea.

And he did. He touched her, and she trembled. He touched her again, and he trembled himself. How seductive it was to feel a man tremble in her arms and know that she was the cause, Caroline realized. How seductive was the heat of his flesh, the texture of his golden skin, the strength of his muscular body.

"I think our curiosity has finally gotten the better of us," Austin muttered as he drew back for a moment, his breathing labored. "What do you say now, Mrs. Douglas? There's no heady wine. No romantic firelight. No more excuses."

"We're still snowed in together," she pointed out, her own breath coming hard and fast.

"Give it up, Caroline," he urged, his voice a throaty rumble. "We both know the truth now."

"And what is the truth?" she asked.

He looked intently into her eyes. "The truth is you melt in my arms when I kiss you." He took her mouth in a drugging kiss that more than proved his point. "The truth is you tremble when I touch you." His fingertips skimmed the curve of her ear, the soft white skin of her neck, the tip of her breast as it visibly puckered under her clothes. And, indeed, she trembled.

She took up the incantation. "The truth is your heart pumps furiously in your chest and your skin grows damp when we kiss, when we touch, Austin Perry." She undid the top two or three buttons of his shirt and slipped her hands inside. She could feel his heart pounding beneath her palm. His skin was moist. "The truth is your eyes get even bluer and your mouth even hungrier if I brush my lips across yours." She did just that, and she was proved right on both counts.

"I don't understand it, but you arouse me as no other woman has," he admitted, and somehow Caroline knew he was telling her the truth. She could certainly feel the evidence of his arousal pressing against her.

She had no memory of unbuttoning the rest of his shirt or of Austin pushing hers aside, yet they must have in the passion of the moment, for they found themselves half nude, their clothes in a tangle between their bodies. He was hot to the touch and she even hotter. Caroline realized she was shaking, and her skin was sleek and wet.

She opened her eyes and saw his dark head con-
trasted with her pale skin. Her breasts were completely
bared. They swelled in anticipation, her nipples hard-
ening almost painfully as he traced an erotic pattern
around and around and over them. She could feel each
breath of his stirring the fine blond down on her arms,
and she shivered. Then his mouth trailed a line of fire
over the smooth planes of her rib cage, his hair tickling
her breasts, the day's growth of beard a sensuous abra-
sive where his chin grazed her nipple. She could feel the
virile strength of his legs beneath her weight. His body
was aroused and inviting; it excited hers in return.

His hands delved behind her and found the small of
her back, urging her closer. She arched into him. Her
eyes flew open when she felt the light, oh, so light, touch
of his tongue on the very tip of her breast.

She cried out. "Austin!"

He chanted her name against her yielding flesh.
"Caroline. Caroline. Caroline."

She watched, unable to tear her eyes away, as he
caught first one nipple and then the other between his
teeth and tugged gently. The sensation was half pain,
half pleasure, and it washed over her in waves such as
she had never known before.

Then she dove between them with one hand to re-
lieve the buttons digging into her skin and bone, and
she inadvertently brushed against his thigh. She heard
him inhale sharply. Taking a deep breath, she tentatively traced with her fingertips the hard, erect con-
tour through his corduroy slacks.

Austin raised his head and stared into her eyes, eyes
dark with unspoken emotion. "I need to touch you. I

have to touch you," he ground out through his teeth, his hand going to the brass button at the waist of her jeans.

Caroline held her breath when she felt his hand between their bodies, pushing into hers. There was something incredibly erotic about his hand melded to hers as both pressed into his body and the wild, damp heat of hers. His palm moved between her legs, caressing the mound of bone and flesh, and she knew he could feel her response right through her Levi's. She couldn't disguise it.

Austin traced the line of her waist and the tiny, idented circle of her navel, his fingers trailing over her softly rounded abdomen, easing down the zipper of her jeans. Then those fingers tangled in the soft brown curls that veed between her thighs, and she could not breathe.

Caroline lifted her head and met his impassioned gaze with her own, and they both realized how close they were to the point of no return. She could see the smoky desire in his darkening eyes, and she knew he could see the passion, the desire, the utter vulnerability in her own. It had been so long since a man had aroused her as this man did with his kiss, his caresses. Perhaps it had been too long. Perhaps other women could abandon themselves to a night of physical passion and satiated satisfaction and greet the morning with no regrets, but Caroline wasn't sure she was one of them. Sex was supposed to be a natural part of life. That's what books and magazines, TV and the movies tried to tell everyone. Sex. Except in dreams, dreams she only occasionally even remembered, it hadn't played an active role in her life for years. She was a little rusty when it came to sharing that part, that much of herself, with a man.

Austin's hand grew still. Caroline knew he could sense her hesitation. He slowly took his hand away and raised it to her face. Her skin was burning, and she was trembling from head to toe. She knew it. Now Austin knew it, as well.

"I want to make love to you," he said quietly, simply.

"And I want to make love with you." They could both almost hear the "but" in her voice. "But just because we want to make love doesn't mean that we should." She lowered her head and then raised it again. "I'm sorry, Austin. I didn't mean for it to go this far."

"First me, now you," he observed with an ironic smile.

"First me, now you?" She failed to understand the point he was making.

"Last night I was the one who called it quits. Tonight it's apparently your turn."

She could see in his eyes what he had obviously seen in hers last night: a desire so strong that caution, common sense, reason—they meant nothing in comparison. Clutching at her disheveled clothing with both hands, she slipped off his lap. She leaned against the kitchen counter for support and forced the air in and out of her lungs. "You are a dangerous man, Austin Perry," she said as she turned to face him.

He got to his feet and walked toward her. He took her face in his hands again. There was a deep-burning fire in his eyes; a belated tremor shot through his body.

"And *you* are a very dangerous woman, Caroline Douglas."

He dropped his hands and moved away from her then. The heavily charged, sensuous atmosphere in the room slowly dissipated as they concentrated on putting their clothes to rights.

It was some time later when Caroline realized that something in the air had changed. Something inside the log cabin. Something outside the cabin. She inclined her head for a moment and then said, "The wind's stopped blowing."

Austin cocked his head to one side, listening. Then he nodded decisively. "That means we'll be able to plow our way out of here tomorrow."

"We'll be able to leave," Caroline murmured as if she didn't quite believe it.

The expression Austin Perry turned on her bore more than a trace of apology. "It's a good thing, too." And his eyes were as blue as she had ever seen them.

5

AT HER AGE, CAROLINE had never expected to find herself reading James Fenimore Cooper's *The Deerslayer*. She'd hated it in her high school English Lit class. In fact, instead she had cheated for the first and only time in school and read the Classic comic-book version of the tales of Leatherstocking and his brother in arms, Chingachgook. She found she was only slightly more tolerant of Cooper's pedantic writing style now, some twenty years later.

She sighed and sat up a little straighter in her chair, the book lying open on her lap. It was either Cooper's novel or one of a dozen copies of *Sports Illustrated*, circa 1981. Austin didn't maintain an extensive library here in his cabin in the mountains. Nor was there anything as technologically advanced as a television or a radio, certainly. When he decided to get away from it all, Austin Perry apparently got away from it *all*.

The front door of the log cabin opened and slammed shut again. Caroline put the book aside and stood up as Austin came into the room, stamping his feet and shaking the snow from the turned-up collar of his sheepskin coat. He brought the sting of frigid morning air in with him and the clean scent of the pine forest.

He yanked his gloves off and loosened the top button or two of his coat before he exclaimed, "Boy, it's cold out there!"

She looked past him to one of the unshuttered windows at the front of the cabin. "It looks cold," she said, and shivered.

He blew on his fingers and rubbed his hands together in an effort to warm them. "Are you ready to go?" he asked.

"All I have to do is put my jacket on and walk out the front door."

"Good." He gestured toward the worn leather volume on the table beside her. "You can take that with you if you'd like to finish reading it."

Caroline glanced down at the book. "Thanks, anyway, but I already know how the story ends." She watched his eyebrows arch in an unspoken question and confessed, "I read the Classic comic-book version in high school."

Austin put his head back, and the room filled with his laughter. "You, too? I have to admit those Classics were the only way I could make it through some of the so-called classics." Then he returned to the business at hand. "The Jeep's warmed up. I put a couple of blankets in the back seat just in case you get cold between here and Keystone."

"How do the roads look?" she asked. He must know by now. He'd been out plowing the gravel drive between the cabin and the mountain road for most of the morning.

Rubbing his hand back and forth along the scruff of his neck, he finally admitted, "I've seen worse."

"That doesn't sound very promising to me," Caroline said as she put on her jacket and gloves. The wool blazer was a mass of wrinkles, and the leather gloves were stiff and cracked in places, but she'd have to change once they got to Keystone, anyway. After wearing the same clothes for three days in a row, she felt as if she never wanted to see them again. "I'm as ready as I'll ever be," she announced, taking several steps toward the door. Then she stopped. "Where's Jake?"

"You don't have to worry about old Jake. He's a survivor from way back," Austin assured her.

Then he smiled at her, and there was that astonishing transformation again. It caught Caroline off guard and left her a little bewildered. This man held an attraction for her that she simply didn't understand, but her instinct for survival warned her that he was dangerous. She'd recognized that on some level from the moment they'd met.

"Where did you say Jake was?" She couldn't seem to remember what he'd said.

"He's already in the Jeep," Austin explained again. "I'm sure he doesn't want to be left behind by some oversight."

"I can't say I blame him," she murmured.

"There are a couple of last-minute things I need to take care of before we leave," he told her as he turned in the direction of the kitchen. "You stay put. I'll be ready to go in less than five minutes."

"Yessir!" Caroline mouthed behind his back. She didn't dare mock the man to his face. He was a whole lot bigger than she was, and he was her ticket out of here.

While she waited for him, she looked around the room. She wasn't sorry to be leaving here, but she knew she would never forget the hours and the days she'd spent in this secluded cabin. Of course, Caroline thought with a sigh, without the warmth of a fire in the fireplace and Austin's larger-than-life presence in the room, it was just a nicely furnished, rather rustic log cabin.

A tear appeared in the corner of her eye. She sniffed and wiped it away. She'd been so emotional the past few days. Her spirits would soar one minute and then take a nosedive the next. She felt as though she were on some kind of roller-coaster ride. To compound the problem, all the primitive urges seemed to have surfaced in this primitive setting: hunger, thirst, sex and survival. It was life reduced to its simplest form. Yet there was nothing simple about her feelings for Austin Perry.

While there was no denying she found him attractive, she tried to tell herself she was a mature woman, the mother of a ten-year-old boy, not some impressionable young girl to be swept off her feet by the first pair of broad shoulders to come along. After all, it wasn't as if she had an overwhelming desire to kiss every man she met. Just the opposite was true. She was very careful around men. In fact, she was downright cautious. So how was she to explain her reaction to this man? Or was it a case of "Fools give you reasons, wise men never try?"

She wanted even now to put her hand on his arm, to draw him down beside her in front of a crackling fire, to light anew the raging flame that would race through their veins, to drive away the demons that plagued her in the still, silent hours of the night.

She wanted to feel his touch on the throbbing pulse at the base of her throat. To feel his hand capture her breast as he counted the beats of her heart. To know his caress on the smooth, silky skin of her abdomen. To have his kiss command her mouth, his tongue seduce hers into warm willingness.

She wanted his hands on her in small, intimate ways. She wanted him all around her and deep, deep inside her. She wanted to know the thrill of his possession, to be his, utterly and completely. A violent, almost orgasmic, shudder racked her body at the picture of him forming in her mind.

Caroline clenched her hand into a fist, her fingernails digging into the soft flesh of her palm as her hand came down hard on the back of the sofa. The same sofa where they had been together, their arms around each other. The memory of the past two nights, of those impassioned moments, flooded her mind and awakened her body.

Could something have happened to her out there in the storm? Something that had melted the deep freeze in which she'd put her sexual feelings and physical needs all these years? Or was it Austin who inspired her to take chances when she had never dared to before, to dream the dreams of a woman who wants, who desires, who loves a living, breathing man?

He was right about one thing, Caroline realized as he walked back into the room. The sensual tension was there between them, even in the cold, harsh light of day. They were wary of each other this morning, and rightly so. Perhaps they were afraid they had revealed too much of themselves this weekend. Perhaps he was as embarrassed as she was to have been swept off his feet. They both had behaved impulsively, indiscreetly, foolishly. It was almost unforgivable at their age.

"It's time to go," Austin prompted, buttoning his sheepskin coat and pulling his gloves on. "I suppose you'll be glad to get out of here this morning," he remarked casually.

"This isn't the way I'd planned to spend my weekend," she reminded him. "But your cabin was a godsend."

"Yes, a godsend," he murmured. "I think I would have gone crazy a long time ago if I hadn't had this place to . . ." His voice trailed off as he searched for the right word.

"To escape to?"

"I suppose escape is as good a word as any." Then, "We better get going." He stared down at her riding boots and frowned. "The snow's pretty deep out there, so stick to the path I've shoveled from here to the Jeep."

He swung open the cabin door. A blast of arctic air hit Caroline squarely in the face. For an agonizing instant it stole her breath away. She forced the cold in and out of her oxygen-starved lungs. Once she could breathe again, she quickly put her head down and covered her mouth with the tail end of her wool scarf, then took her first step into the wintry Colorado morning. The door was closed behind her with a resounding finality, the key turned in the lock. There would be no going back now.

She found herself sticking to the shoveled path as she'd been instructed. It seemed an eternity before she looked up and saw the Jeep in front of her and Austin opening the door on the passenger's side.

"Thank you!" she called out as she took a step up and settled herself in the seat. He closed the door behind her, and that was when she finally took a deep breath, grateful for the warm air inside the vehicle.

It took her several minutes to go through the ritual of rearranging the scarf around her neck, of running her fingers through her disheveled hair, of turning to notice that Jake was sitting on the seat behind them. He seemed unperturbed by it all, even by the army-green blankets and several good-sized plastic garbage bags stacked around him in the rear of the Jeep.

"Better fasten your seat belt," Austin barked at her as he got in the driver's side. "We could be in for a rough ride."

She pulled the strap across her body and dutifully latched the metal buckle in place. Austin turned the key in the ignition, put the four-wheel drive into gear and started off down the driveway. It wasn't long before they reached the mountain road, and he lowered the plow attached to the front of the Jeep.

"It's going to be slow going from here on out," he warned her as they started down the mountain.

Caroline sat back and stared out the window in front of her. That's when she realized it was almost impossible to tell where the road was. It was all one big expanse of white in front of them! She took in a breath and held it as they approached what was evidently the first bend in the winding road. God alone knew how Austin managed to execute the turn. She sat there, clenching her teeth until they hurt.

"How—" The word came out as a high-pitched squeak, an octave higher than her normal voice. She swallowed the lump in her throat and tried again. "How do you know where the road is?"

Austin kept his eyes straight ahead. "I've driven this road a hundred times."

That's what she'd been afraid he was going to say— he was making a serious error if he thought that's what she wanted to hear. She preferred something a bit more substantial to cling to than the knowledge that he was driving solely from memory!

She took a deep breath and let it out slowly. "Do you think this is a good idea?"

"Would you prefer to stay holed up in the cabin until the next thaw?" he asked bluntly.

That effectively shut her up. The mountain road was knee-deep in snow. The journey was going to be treacherous. Caroline could feel the oversize tires dig down a foot or more to grab at the gravel buried beneath the snow. The Jeep slid precariously close to the edge of the road when they hit a patch of ice. Her back went rigid against the seat. There was a dull ache behind her eyes as she stared straight ahead of her, as if by the sheer force of her will she could keep the vehicle safely on the road.

Her mouth was dry, her palms wet inside her leather gloves. She experienced a sudden, awful vertigo, and her stomach lurched sickeningly. The wind came up. It was blowing furiously across their path. The mountains loomed in front of them and all around them, silent and regal and arrogant.

Caroline turned her head and stared out the window on her side of the Jeep. She gave a small hiss when she spotted a telltale white cloud rising from the next mountain. It was an avalanche, if only a minor one, and no threat to them. She had seen the real thing once. It had been an awesome sight, inspiring that mixed feeling of reverence, fear and wonder at the power of nature here in the Rockies, where even the biggest man was dwarfed by his surroundings.

Yes, an avalanche could be a devastating force. Hundreds and thousands of tons of white destruction roaring down the face of a mountain, sweeping it bare of trees and brush, boulders and whatever life dared to get in its way. Great chunks of compacted snow suffocating and swamping and hurling and grinding into bits before burying everything in an icy barrage. Caroline didn't think she would ever forget the sight.

"It's not headed in our direction, but there is a small avalanche in the next valley," she turned to tell Austin.

There were tiny beads of perspiration on the man's brow and upper lip. He didn't bother wiping them away. His eyes were fixed to the road ahead. "There have been as many as two hundred and twenty-five avalanches reported in these mountains on a single Sunday," he stated in a tutorial tone.

Caroline didn't find that a particularly comforting thought. She gritted her teeth as the Jeep slid from side to side on the slippery road. She took a deep breath and began to hum softly to herself.

"What are you humming?" Austin inquired without turning his head. "It sounds like a funeral dirge."

"It's not. It's 'L'inverno,' the fourth concerto from Vivaldi's *The Four Seasons*."

"'L'inverno'?" He surprised her by pronouncing it correctly.

"Yes, 'Winter,'" she translated.

"Do you know anything by the Supremes?"

Caroline laughed outright. The sound of her laughter filled the Jeep, then died a quick death as they suddenly swerved to miss a tree lying halfway across the road. The slender aspen was splintered around the trunk some six feet up from the ground, no doubt at the point where the weight of the snow had broken it in half. She felt her body strain against the seat belt as she was thrown forward and then back. She instinctively put her hand out to cushion the blow.

"Are you all right?" Austin called out as he regained control of the wheel.

She nodded. "I'm fine."

"Jake?"

They both turned at the same instant. Although Austin's attention necessarily reverted to the road,

Caroline watched as Jake picked himself up off the floor of the back seat with as much dignity as he could muster under the circumstances. He jumped up on the seat and sat there staring at them, his inscrutable green eyes narrowed into two slits. Then he deliberately turned his back on them and began to groom himself.

Caroline tried to sound cheerful. "It looks like Jake's all right. Other than being slightly put out with us, of course."

Austin shot her a quick sideways glance. "Then let's see if we can get to the main road without another incident."

"How does it look ahead?" she asked tentatively.

"You can see for yourself." He sounded more than a little doubtful as they plowed through the snow.

"What's all that stuff for in the back seat?" She had spotted an old army shovel and several large plastic bags behind Jake.

"The shovel is to dig with, and the bags of ashes from the fireplace are to put under the tires for added traction in case we get stuck." His smile was strained. "By the way, have you ever driven a standard shift?"

She shrugged her shoulders noncommittally. "Of course I have. A boyfriend of mine had a car with a standard shift. He used to let me drive it once in a while."

"How long ago was that?" Austin asked with some reluctance.

"Back when I was in high school," she said, knowing that wasn't the answer he wanted to hear.

It wasn't. Austin shook his head. "Then we better hope and pray you don't have to drive."

They wound their way carefully down the mountain. It was a half hour or more before they noticed that the snow alongside the road was starting to thin out.

"I think we're going to make it!" Caroline cried out happily.

"Yes, but I don't mind telling you now that I wasn't sure for a while back there." He laughed, obviously relieved. "Whew, I'm hot, if you can believe that!" He tore off his gloves and tried to unbutton his sheepskin coat.

"Here, let me do that for you." Caroline reached across and undid the buttons. Then she helped him off with his coat and tossed it in the back. She caught Austin's eye as she turned, and her expression sobered immediately. "We were lucky, weren't we?"

"Damn lucky," he admitted in the softest voice she had heard him use yet. A few minutes later they pulled up to the intersection where the mountain road met the paved highway. "It doesn't look like they got as much snow down here," he observed, easing the Jeep up to a stop sign.

"The snowplows have been through here, too," Caroline added, distracted by her own thoughts. It had suddenly occurred to her that this was the end of the journey for them. Austin Perry was going to drop her off at her car and drive away. That would be the end of it. And what would she be left with? Half of a dream, a dream of love that never had been?

"Where are you parked?" he asked as they drove into Keystone.

"Turn left at the next intersection. There's my car." She raised her arm and pointed toward the parking lot alongside the stables.

Austin slowed down and pulled off to one side of the highway. "That's your car?" His inquisitive gaze focused on the full-size family station wagon buried in a snowdrift up to its bumpers.

"Yes. I drive a station wagon because I'm in a lot of car pools. I'm always driving a den or a troop or a team somewhere," she explained. "It's a fact of suburban life."

He grunted, and his brows met in a thoughtful scowl. "The snowplows have done a fine job of burying your car. We'll have to dig you out, of course. I'll get the shovel."

It took him twenty minutes or more to clear away enough of the snow for Caroline to have a chance of moving her station wagon. She took the keys from her jeans pocket and unlocked the door on the driver's side. Sliding across the front seat, she opened the glove compartment and retrieved her purse and the keys to her parents' condominium.

Then she settled herself behind the steering wheel, inserted the key in the ignition and turned it. Nothing happened. She tried again. And again nothing happened.

Austin stuck his head through the open window. "What seems to be the trouble?"

"Talk about the last straw," she grumbled, swearing under her breath. "It won't start!"

"Here, let me try," he said, opening the door.

"I don't usually have this much trouble with cars and things," she stated in her own defense. She wasn't convinced he could do any better, but let the man try if he was so sure of himself.

"Sometimes it takes just the right touch," Austin informed her as he turned the key in the ignition. Nothing happened. He tried several more times, and each time he met with the same results. He opened the door and swung his long legs out of the car, all the while muttering under his breath. He walked around to the front of the station wagon and raised the hood. Bending over, he stared at the engine.

Caroline knew the technical terms for everything under the hood of her car—a single woman had to know a carburetor from a catalytic converter these days in order to protect herself—but it was all still gobbledygook to her when something went wrong.

"Well, Dr. Perry, what's your diagnosis?" she asked with a wry smile, leaning over the front of the automobile and sticking her head down beside his.

He looked at the grease on his hands, took a white handkerchief from his back pocket, wiped his hands clean and stuffed the greasy hanky back from whence it came. "The battery seems to have lost its charge," he announced soberly.

"Huh?"

"You've got a dead battery."

"Well, it'll just have to get undead," she proclaimed stubbornly. "I've got to get back to Denver this afternoon."

Austin studied a dark streak down the back of his hand that he'd somehow missed with the handkerchief. Then he looked up at her and asked, "And who do you think you're going to find to charge a dead battery in this kind of weather and on a Sunday afternoon? We've just been through an unexpected major snowstorm. There must be dead batteries lined up from one end of this state to the other." His eyes grew thoughtful. "You don't happen to belong to a motor club, do you?"

Caroline kicked at the right front tire in frustration. "No, I don't."

"Then I suggest that you let me handle this," Austin remarked confidently. "I'll drive you to Denver after you've had a chance to get your things from your parents' condominium. Then we'll go to the airport to pick up your parents and your son."

"But that's a terrible imposition," she protested.

He dismissed her objection with a wave of his hand. "Consider it fair payment for the thirty-seven dollars and fifty-three cents I owe you."

She cast him a skeptical look. "What about my car?"

"It will only take a couple of telephone calls once I get to my office in the morning. I'll arrange to have someone charge up the battery and deliver the car to you in Denver by tomorrow afternoon." He closed the hood of the station wagon and took her elbow firmly. "We'll lock it up and leave it right here. By the way, you might want to leave a note for the old wrangler. Then while you're changing or packing or whatever you need to do at your parents', I'll call the stable owners' office at Keystone and let them know you're all right and that your car will be out of here no later than noon tomorrow."

"Are you always this—organized?" Caroline laughed, amazed.

"Yes." Austin flashed her a dazzling smile. "I'm told it's part of my charm." Then he was all business again. "What time does your parents' plane get into Stapleton?"

"Five o'clock," she answered, glancing down at her watch.

He responded with a well-organized and thoroughly charming, "Let's get a move on."

It was precisely five minutes to five when they pulled into the parking lot at Denver's Stapleton Airport.

6

AUSTIN WATCHED AS CAROLINE went up on her tiptoes for the tenth time in as many minutes. The airplane was late, but just barely. The flight from Orlando, routed through Atlanta, was due momentarily. He didn't understand why she was so anxious, but she was.

"There it is!" Caroline exclaimed as she pointed toward the jumbo jet taxiing into the terminal area. She moved closer to the gate where the plane was scheduled to unload.

It was another five minutes before the passengers started to empty through the door. Austin stood behind her, his hands resting lightly on her shoulders. He inhaled deeply. She smelled of freshly shampooed hair and some pretty heady perfume. Suddenly he minded even less that she'd taken time to shower at her parents' condominium earlier that afternoon.

"What's that scent you're wearing?" he asked in a husky voice as he took another deep breath.

Caroline turned and looked up at him, a puzzled expression on her face. She was obviously having trouble hearing him over the noise of the crowd and the public-address system. "What did you say?"

"I said, what's that perfume you're wearing?"

"My perfume? White Shoulders."

How appropriate, he thought, remembering her soft white skin. At that moment he felt her muscles tense beneath his hands, and he looked up toward the open door. A man and a woman, both in their sixties, were walking into the terminal. A boy was with them. "Is that your family?" he asked, suddenly curious.

"Yes." The fullness in her voice betrayed her. He knew she was on the verge of tears, and he gave her shoulders a squeeze.

Austin studied the threesome coming toward them through the crowd. The man was handsomely graying and trim but shorter than Austin had expected. There was little doubt that his daughter would tower over him if she chose to wear high heels. His brightly colored knit golf shirt and casual slacks seemed out of place amid Denver's wintry ice and snow.

The stylish woman on his arm was nearly as tall as he was. She was attractive and still slender, her dark brown hair sprinkled with silver. Her complexion was creamy. If she wore any makeup, it was expertly applied. Her eyes—Austin found that her eyes were impossible to describe. They had that same beautifully elusive quality as her daughter's. This was what Caroline would look like in another twenty years or so, he realized, and smiled to himself. It was undoubtedly a high recommendation.

A lighter brown and slightly curly head of hair popped up between the two adults. This was her son, Austin had to remind himself. This tall, tanned, long-legged kid on the brink of adolescence was Caroline's son. Somehow he'd expected Jeremy—yes, that was his name, Jeremy—to be more of a boy and less of a young man.

He bent over and brushed the curve of her ear with his lips as he asked, "How long has your son been away?"

"Jeremy has been visiting my parents in Florida for the past ten days. We've never been separated for that long before. I thought it might be good for both of us," she said impatiently.

Her impatience made her seem uncertain, Austin thought, dropping his hands to his sides as she moved a step or two away from him. He wondered if she still felt the separation had been such a good idea.

The boy was the first one to make it through the crowd. He came up to his mother and planted a self-conscious kiss on her cheek. "Hi, Mom."

"Jeremy—" It was all she could manage before her arms went around his lanky body, pressing his light brown head to her breast.

"Hello, dear, here we are at last," said the woman who came up behind her grandson just as he managed to break free. She bestowed a maternal kiss on Caroline's cheek and thrust a bag of oranges into her hands. "Oranges from Florida. After all, everybody expects them." She laughed, sounding a little tired.

"How was your flight, Mother?" Caroline shifted the sack of citrus fruit in her arms and didn't wait for an answer. "Hello, Dad." She turned to the man waiting patiently behind his wife.

"Caroline, my dear." He put his arms around her and held her for a moment. Then he reached out to encom-

pass his wife and grandson. "We're all here together."
He was obviously moved and more than a little pleased.

"Yes, we're all here together," Caroline agreed, turning at the last minute to include Austin in their family group. "I'd like you to meet a—a friend of mine. This is Austin Perry." She had stumbled over the word "friend" but made a nice recovery, Austin thought. "Austin, this is my mother and father, Edna and Harry Davis, and my son, Jeremy."

"Mrs. Davis, this is indeed a pleasure. Mr. Davis." He came forward and acknowledged each of her parents with a firm handshake. Then he turned to the boy. Jeremy Douglas took his hand and looked up at him for the first time, and Austin was thrown for a real loop. Why hadn't Caroline told him? Why hadn't she warned him? He had almost had a heart attack. For there, staring up into his blue eyes, were the almost identical blue eyes of her son! "I, ah, I understand you've been vacationing in Florida," he finally managed.

"Yessir. I've been to Disney World, Epcot, Sea World, the Space Center and the beach. My grandparents took me. It's not too far from their condominium at Daytona Beach." He turned back to his mother. "Florida was great, Mom!"

"I can't wait to hear all about it." She laughed with delight at his enthusiasm. "I take it you had a good time at Disney World."

He grinned boyishly. The kind of grin a mother no doubt quickly learned to cherish. "It was tough!"

"Now that is a compliment," Caroline said in an aside to Austin. "'Tough' is usually reserved for his favorite rock singer." She turned to her mother. "Did you have a good flight?" Then she laughed. "Have I asked you that question already?"

"Yes to both of your questions," replied Edna Davis as they started toward the baggage-claim area. "But I didn't have the opportunity to answer you, dear. We did have a good flight. It was a bit long but smooth for a change."

"Any flight that's uneventful is a good flight, in my opinion," declared Harry Davis as he walked beside Austin, trying to match his stride with that of the man who towered over him by a good six inches or more.

"I'm in complete agreement with you, Harry," Caroline heard Austin say to her father. She wondered just when and how the two men had gotten on a first-name basis.

She raised her voice just enough to be heard above the noise all around them. "We'll get the luggage, Mother, and then Austin has volunteered to get his Jeep so you won't have to walk far in this weather. We had a snowstorm here over the weekend, you know."

"Mr. Perry's Jeep?"

"Austin's Jeep?" Astonishment was voiced as one by Edna and Harry Davis.

"A Jeep? A real Jeep? Tough!" chimed in Jeremy.

"Where is your car, dear?" asked her mother.

"I'm afraid my station wagon is snowed in up at Keystone with a dead battery. It's a long story, but Austin was nice enough to drive me back to the city and even come to the airport to pick you up. I don't know what I would have done without him," she said, scarcely realizing the significance of what she was admitting until it was too late.

"I'm glad you're beginning to realize how indispensable I can be," Austin murmured as they trooped on through the airport toward the baggage claim.

Caroline fixed a careful smile on her mouth and turned to her parents. "You'll want to put your coats on even for the short walk outside. The high in Denver today was thirty degrees."

"And to think it was nearly eighty degrees when we left our hotel in Orlando this morning," Edna Davis commented as she slipped on the fur jacket she'd been carrying over her arm. "Tell me, dear," she whispered to her daughter some ten minutes later as Austin arrived curbside with his Jeep, "what in the world is that *creature* sitting in Mr. Perry's back seat? It's staring at us."

"That's Jake, Mother, Austin's cat," Caroline explained as she gingerly picked up the tomcat and held him close to her. Meanwhile Austin and her father loaded the suitcases into the back of the four-door Cherokee.

From there Austin took over. Caroline was genuinely grateful for the man's consideration. "Why don't you sit in the front, Mrs. Davis? I think you'll find it more comfortable."

"Thank you, Mr. Perry," Edna Davis responded politely as he assisted her up into the Jeep.

"Please call me Austin," he urged with all his considerable charm and masculine persuasion. He was a sly one. Caroline sighed as she watched her own mother fall victim to his charms. It seemed no woman was immune. All it took was a little attention from a handsome man.

She turned to her father and her son. "I guess that leaves the back seat for us, guys."

Once they were all inside and the doors were closed, Caroline released her hold on Jake. She was surprised when the usually aloof tomcat chose to remain on her lap. She didn't know what it was, but she'd surmised there was something or someone in Jake's background that had left him feeling ill-disposed toward women. Normally he avoided her like the plague.

She heard Austin ask her son what he'd liked best about Disney World. Jeremy responded eagerly. That was something of a surprise to her, as well. Jeremy hadn't always taken kindly to the few men she'd tried to have as friends since his father's death. Some people said it was jealousy on his part, but she knew better. It wasn't jealousy; it was simply that her son felt fiercely protective of her.

"My favorites were the Jungle Cruise, the Pirates of the Caribbean, the submarine ride and the Big Thunder Mountain Railroad. That's a roller coaster. I rode on it six times yesterday. And I liked the race cars they let you drive all by yourself," he told Austin.

"What did you think of Epcot?" Caroline asked.

"It was neat! Especially some of the stuff in Future World." Jeremy could barely contain his excitement. "There was this one attraction in the Universe of Energy where you rode in a moving theater. It took you into a forest where there were dinosaurs and big birds that could fly, and earthquakes and volcanoes. They said it had something called smell-a-rama. It really smelled like an old rain forest millions of years ago, too."

Caroline wrinkled her nose and remarked to her father, "Your feet must be worn out."

"Thank goodness there were a lot of attractions you could ride through," Harry said dryly.

"The thing that impressed me the most was the cleanliness of the place and how friendly and well organized everyone was," Edna Davis said. "You would have enjoyed the World Showcase, Caroline. It was like a bigger and better world's fair, with numerous countries represented on a permanent basis."

"I'm sure I would have. Maybe I'll have a chance to see it the next time I get to Florida."

Edna turned her attention to the man behind the steering wheel. "Have you ever been to Florida, Mr. Perry?"

"No, I'm afraid I haven't, Mrs. Davis." He flashed her one of his brilliant smiles. "I thought you were going to call me Austin."

She glanced at his corduroy pants and his flannel shirt and those dreadful army boots he insisted on wearing, then inquired, "What do you do, Austin?"

"I'm the CEO of the Perry Mining Company, Mrs. Davis," he replied with a modicum of modesty.

"That probably means you're the president of the company, right?" Harry said approvingly.

NOW THAT THE DOOR IS OPEN...
Peel off the bouquet and send it on the postpaid order card to receive:

T.M.

4 FREE BOOKS!
An attractive burgundy umbrella—FREE!
And a mystery gift as an EXTRA BONUS!

PLUS

MONEY-SAVING HOME DELIVERY!
Once you receive your 4 FREE books and gifts, you'll be able to open your door to more great romance reading month after month. Enjoy the convenience of previewing four brand-new books every month delivered right to your home months before they appear in stores. Each book is yours for only $1.99—26¢ less than the retail price.

SPECIAL EXTRAS—FREE!
You'll get our free monthly newsletter, *Heart to Heart*—the indispensable insider's look at our most popular writers and their upcoming novels. You'll also get additional free gifts from time to time as a token of our appreciation for being a home subscriber.

NO-RISK GUARANTEE
- There's no obligation to buy—and the free books and gifts are yours to keep forever.
- You pay the lowest price possible and receive books months before they appear in stores.
- You may end your subscription anytime—just write and let us know.

RETURN THE POSTPAID ORDER CARD TODAY AND OPEN YOUR DOOR TO THESE 4 EXCITING, LOVE-FILLED NOVELS. THEY ARE YOURS ABSOLUTELY FREE, ALONG WITH YOUR FOLDING UMBRELLA AND MYSTERY GIFT.

HARLEQUIN READER SERVICE
901 Fuhrmann Blvd.,
P.O. Box 1394,
Buffalo, NY 14240-9963.

Place the Bouquet here →

Yes! I have attached the bouquet above. Please send me my four Harlequin Temptation® novels, free, along with my free folding umbrella and mystery gift. Then send me four new Harlequin Temptation® novels every month as they come off the presses, and bill me just $1.99 per book (26¢ less than retail), with no extra charges for shipping and handling. If I am not completely satisfied, I may return a shipment and cancel at any time. The free books and gifts remain mine to keep.

142 CIX MDMR

Name _____

Address _____ Apt. _____

City _____ Province/State _____

Postal Code/Zip _____

Offer limited to one per household and not valid for present subscribers. Prices subject to change.

PRINTED IN U.S.A.

Take this beautiful
FOLDING UMBRELLA
with your 4 FREE BOOKS
PLUS A MYSTERY GIFT

If order card is missing, write to Harlequin Reader Service,
901 Fuhrmann Blvd., P.O. Box 1394, Buffalo, NY 14240-9963.

Caroline watched her mother turn toward the younger man and insist, "Please call me Edna. Is your company into gold and silver mining, Austin?"

If he was offended by her sudden show of interest, Austin Perry certainly wasn't acting that way. "We mine some silver and gold, Edna, but Perry Mining is mostly into the non-precious metals at this stage: tungsten, vanadium, molybdenum and uranium."

"Uranium?" Caroline could almost hear the wheels turning in her mother's head.

"Yes, uranium. Of course, the importance of uranium wasn't understood when the company was founded by my great-grandfather back before the turn of the century. In those days we were predominantly into gold and silver mining. My father took over when his father died after the Second World War. He added a number of other mines to the family's holdings. I became president when my father retired five years ago. I already had my own mining concerns, so we merged the whole operation." He was forced to stop talking as he drove up to the exit of the airport parking lot.

"That'll be two dollars, sir," the attendant informed him in a brisk, businesslike tone.

Edna moved their conversation into new territory as soon as the parking fee was paid and they were on the highway headed toward Caroline's house. "Has my daughter told you about the success of her own business? I must confess that even Harry and I have been surprised by how well she's done for herself."

Austin gave it a moment's thought before answering. "Yes, she's mentioned that she has done rather well with Christmas by Caroline."

"You would be astonished by the money to be made in one-of-a-kind and antique Christmas decorations." Edna shook her head and made a small clucking sound not unlike that of a mother hen. "And to think it all started with Caroline's hobby of collecting antique ornaments and making wax figures from old molds. Who would have thought? Now, of course, the best artisans in six states work for her. Yes, she's developed quite a talent for knowing what the public will buy." Then Edna shrugged her elegant shoulders as if to say it was only natural that her daughter would be a success.

"I'm sure you and Harry have every right to be proud of Caroline's business acumen," Austin said with a smile.

"Yes, we are. But we're just as proud of the fact that she has never neglected her home or Jeremy in favor of her business," she assured him. "She has always been a homemaker and a mother first, and a darned good one, too."

Caroline felt compelled to speak up from the back seat. She had allowed her mother to go on for too long as it was. "Thank you for the testimonial, Mother, but the next thing we know, you'll be telling Austin what good teeth I have."

Edna Davis could be a remarkably single-minded woman. "But you do have good teeth, dear."

In the end it was Jeremy who spoke up and saved the day. "I'm starved, Mom. When do we get to eat?"

With that, they launched into an animated discussion of food, specifically airline food. This kept them on a nice safe topic for the rest of the drive home.

EDNA OPENED the hall closet door in her daughter's turn-of-the-century home and slipped off her fur jacket. She reached for a coat hanger and lowered her voice to a theatrical whisper. "I thought I should say something to you, dear, while the men are carrying the suitcases upstairs. Aren't we going to invite Austin to join us for dinner? I think it's the least we can do when he was kind enough to bring us home from the airport. Not to mention driving you all the way down from Keystone."

"Of course we'll issue him an invitation for dinner if you think we should," Caroline concurred, silently grinding her teeth together.

If only her mother didn't feel it was still her duty to remind her on a regular basis about "proper" etiquette. Of course she should have thought to invite Austin to dinner herself. Surely she would have if she hadn't felt so flustered during the drive from the airport to her house. Sometimes her mother had all the finesse of a Sherman tank when it came to matchmaking. If there was an eligible male within thirty miles, she sprang into action. And Austin Perry was undoubtedly an eligible male in Edna Davis's book.

"I'm sure I would have invited Austin to join us for dinner if I hadn't had so many other things on my mind," she finally assured her mother.

The older woman turned a beautifully innocent gaze on the daughter who looked so much like her. "Of course you would have, dear," she said confidently as she closed the closet door.

Caroline opened her mouth, then diplomatically closed it again when she saw Jeremy bounding down the stairs two at a time. Hands and feet, that's what boys were really made of.

"Hey, Mom, can I call Joey while you and Grandma are making dinner? I want to find out if anything happened while I was gone on vacation."

"All right, but you can only talk for ten minutes. Then you get down here and set the dinner table," she said far more sternly than she had intended.

"I can set the table tonight, Caroline. That is, if it's all right with you," Edna volunteered, trying to smooth over the moment.

Caroline permitted herself a small sigh and consciously tried to relax the muscles that had tensed along the back of her neck and across her shoulders. "Okay, Jeremy, you can go ahead and call your friend. I'll let you know when dinner's ready."

She saw her father and Austin coming down the stairs as her son raced back up them, still two at a time. When had Jeremy's legs grown so long, Caroline wondered. He'd soon be needing new jeans again.

"Not only is Keystone offering these package deals for skiers, but Breckenridge, Copper Mountain and Arapahoe have joined in, as well," Harry was saying. "I guess it's good for the economy, but I'm old-fashioned, Austin. I liked Colorado the way it was when Edna and I first came here from the Midwest nearly thirty years ago."

"Times have changed things, Harry. There's no doubt about that," the younger man commiserated.

"Excuse me, gentlemen," Caroline interrupted them as politely as she could under the circumstances. "I don't suppose you would care to join us for dinner tonight, would you, Austin? It won't be anything fancy," she added nervously as he reached the bottom of the stairs.

He'd never seemed quite so tall to her or quite so forbidding as he did at that moment. The look of him sent an odd chill down her spine. Austin Perry was going to be trouble. She just knew it.

He flashed her a broad smile as he strode forward and dropped a lingering kiss on her mouth, as if this were something he did every day—or perhaps every *night*— of the week. "Thanks, honey, I'd love to stay for dinner."

Yes, she knew it! Caroline was furious. He was up to no good! And how dared he kiss her like that in front of her parents? He had to realize that would give them the wrong impression of their relationship. With an awful, sinking feeling, she knew this man was going to give her trouble with a capital *T*.

Her father spoke up. "Don't you worry about Austin and me. We can entertain ourselves while you get dinner on the table. What do you drink, Austin?" he asked as the two men sauntered off in the direction of the family room, Jake at their heels.

"Scotch, no water please, Harry." Caroline overheard Austin's reply as she slammed the kitchen door behind her. She hoped he choked on his Scotch. If there was any justice left in the world, he would, too!

She turned and saw her mother standing there with the refrigerator door open, gazing inside as if she could somehow divine the secrets of the universe from its contents. "Tell me, Caroline, exactly what did you have planned for dinner tonight?"

"There's a big pan of lasagna and a couple of loaves of garlic bread in the freezer. I thought I'd throw together a salad to go with it," she said, trying to calm herself.

"Ah, here it is," Edna exclaimed with apparent relief as she opened the freezer compartment. She took out the lasagna and set it on the kitchen counter. "Do you want to warm both loaves of garlic bread?"

"I think we better. A man the size of Austin Perry is bound to have an appetite to match all that—brawn," Caroline muttered in a sarcastic tone.

"Speaking of Austin, I don't recall your ever mentioning his name before," Edna remarked, oh, so casually as she took a head of lettuce and several tomatoes from the crisper. "When did you two happen to meet?"

Caroline took the pan of lasagna from the counter and put it in the microwave oven. She programmed the baking time and heaved a sigh of resignation before she began to explain. "The reason you've never heard his name before, Mother, is because I just met Austin Perry this weekend." She might as well get it over with and tell her everything. Her mother had an uncanny ability to get the whole truth and nothing but the truth out of her, anyway. "I went horseback riding Friday afternoon up in the mountains above Keystone. The horse threw me and ran off. I was walking back to the stables on foot when I got lost in the mountains." She paused and remembered for a moment, a chill running down her back. "It started to snow. Luckily I stumbled on Austin's cabin, and he took me in until the storm blew over."

Edna Davis turned on the cold water and rinsed the vegetables off before she inquired in a perfectly bland tone, "When was that, dear?"

"Austin drove me down to your place at Keystone this morning," she responded in a carefully schooled voice.

"He drove you down this morning," Edna repeated as she dried the tomatoes with a paper towel and began to slice them into thick wedges. When she was finished, she looked up at her daughter. It was one of those looks that Caroline had come to know well over the years. Her mother was thinking it, if not actually saying it out loud: had she slept with the man? There was an odd expectancy, almost an expression of hope on her mother's face.

Caroline raised an eyebrow and looked away without saying anything. Could this be the same woman whose idea of explaining the facts of life to her sixteen-year-old daughter had been the sole admonishment, "Be careful, darling. Emotions can run high between a boy and a girl"?

Times change, she thought with a sigh. People change. Even her own parents.

"Did you know that a recent study done by a major Ivy League college revealed that there are only sixty-two single men for every one hundred single women between the ages of thirty and thirty-five?" Edna began to tear the lettuce into bite-size pieces. "Take some advice from a woman twice your age—"

"You're not twice my age, Mother. I'm thirty-six, and you're only sixty-one."

Edna waved that consideration aside. "It's close enough. Take my advice and be nice to this Austin Perry. A man like that doesn't come along every day of the week." A crease formed between her perfectly shaped brows. "You're sure he's single, aren't you?"

Caroline frowned, too. "Yes, I'm sure he's single."

Edna went on, oblivious to her daughter's feelings. "As president of his own company, Austin sounds like an excellent financial prospect. He'd be a good provider for you and Jeremy. And he's certainly a handsome man. Why, even my old heart went pitter-patter when I first saw him at the airport tonight." Then she dropped any romantic pretense and became strictly practical. "Let's face it, there aren't that many good prospects knocking on the door at your age."

Caroline turned to her, the color riding high in her face. "Mother, why are you always trying to fix me up with some man?"

The look she got in return was one of pure innocence. "Am I, dear?"

"Yes, you are. I'm sure you remember Mrs. Porter from your Wednesday morning bridge club. What about her son?"

"Johnny Porter was too young for you, dear."

"I know that, Mother." She sighed, realizing she'd failed to make her point. "What about that friend of yours and Daddy's that you brought over for dinner last summer?"

"You must mean Richard Elliot?"

"Yes, that's the one."

"Gracious, Dick Elliot would be too old for you, Caroline. He's the same age as your father," Edna said without blinking an eye. "You'd be much better off with someone Austin's age. How old do you suppose he is?"

Caroline shook her head and started to laugh. It was the only thing she could do. "Mother, you're incorrigible!"

Edna Davis looked at her daughter. "I'm what, dear?"

She went up to the woman and gave her an affectionate hug. "Never mind, Mom. I love you."

"I love you, too, darling," Edna said, picking up the head of cauliflower to prepare it for the salad. "But we'd better get dinner ready before those hungry men of ours come in here looking for it."

Caroline got out the ingredients for the salad dressing and began to mix a variety of herbs and spices with the oil and vinegar. "He's thirty-eight years old."

"Who is thirty-eight years old?" Edna asked as she cleaned the head of cauliflower and broke it into pieces.

"You know who." Several minutes later Caroline added, "I'm very attracted to him."

"Are you, dear?"

"Yes. I don't know what it is about him...." Caroline just stood there, staring off into space.

"It can be like that sometimes between a man and a woman," Edna said without turning her head.

"What should I do?" her daughter blurted out at last.

Her mother didn't say anything for a minute or two. Then she advised, "Give it time. That's the only way to find out if it's more than just a passing fancy."

"I guess you're right."

"I know I am. Time will tell, dear. It always does."

"Yes, time always does," Caroline repeated, regarding her mother with genuine affection as she opened the oven door and placed the loaves of garlic bread on the center rack. Then she checked on the pan of bubbling lasagna....

"LASAGNA AND GARLIC BREAD, how did you know that was one of my favorite meals?" Austin taunted lightly. It was several hours later, and Caroline was walking him to the front door after he'd politely said good-night to her family.

"I didn't know, and you know it," she shot back at him. Then she remembered all that he'd done for her during the past three days, and she relented a little. "You were very nice to Jeremy and my parents. I appreciate that."

"It's not hard to be nice to your family, Caroline. Jeremy is a great kid, and I genuinely like Edna and Harry."

Austin put an arm around her shoulders and drew her closer to him.

"I must apologize for my mother. If she claims she doesn't have time for a hobby, it's because she's too busy matchmaking. I heard the way she was interrogating you during dinner. I imagine she got everything but your shoe size."

Austin tilted her chin up and gazed down at her with a lopsided smile. "Oh, she got that, too. It was while you were in the kitchen refilling the coffeepot."

Caroline groaned. "I'm sorry."

"You don't have to apologize for your mother. I really didn't mind her questions."

She tried to change the subject. "Was it absolutely necessary for you to go into that much detail about this past weekend with my father? If it had happened fifteen or twenty years ago, he would have been after you with a shotgun!"

Austin brought his hands up to rest on her shoulders. Then he gently rubbed his thumb back and forth across her bottom lip. Such a simple gesture, yet it sent shivers straight through her. "Harry and I understand each other perfectly," he murmured.

"That's—" Caroline swallowed hard and tried again "—that's what I'm afraid of."

"You know, I agree with both your parents. You need a good man in your life." He paused and looked into her eyes for a long moment. "I have every intention of being that man, Caroline Douglas."

He caught her face between his palms as his head came down toward hers. "What are you doing?" she asked breathlessly.

"When a man goes prospecting, he never knows when he'll hit an unexpectedly rich vein, what we in the mining business call a mother lode."

She tried to pull away and failed. Lowering her voice, she repeated, "A mother lode?"

"Yes, and like any good miner, I'm staking my claim," he muttered in a husky voice.

Then he kissed her, and the caress gave Caroline both the warmest feeling and the coldest chill down her back that she'd ever felt. Her pulse was a great heartthrob in her throat. When this man kissed her, everything else, everyone else, on the face of the earth simply ceased to exist. He was no good for her. He was the best thing that had ever happened to her.

She felt his hands slide down her shoulders and over her breasts, lingering there for a moment while he savored the feel of her nipples swelling beneath his touch. Then he moved on to her waist and skirted down over her hips. He grasped her buttocks in his hands and pressed her against him. That quickly his body sprang to life. It was clear he wanted her.

"Austin, please, you mustn't!" she whispered frantically.

"I can't help myself," he said tensely. "I've spent the whole lousy day keeping my hands off you, and I can't help myself anymore."

"Please," she repeated, even as her mouth began to move wildly beneath his, even as she arched her body to meet his. "Please, someone may walk in on us." She was trying to reason with him, trying to quell the raging fire that burned inside her. But to no avail, until he grasped her by the hips and she was forced to cry out, "Ouch!"

"Did I hurt you?" he asked, pulling back.

"A little," she admitted. "For some reason the bumps and bruises from my fall seem to be showing up today instead of yesterday."

"You should have told me," he said as the light of reason reignited in his eyes. He tore his mouth from hers as if it pained him physically to do so. His breathing was hard and fast. She was pressed against his chest; she could hear the pandemoniac racing of his life's blood.

The passion between them was as powerful as the spring river churning between the mountains, as unsettling as the storm clouds that glowered over iceshrouded peaks, as fragile as frozen mouse breath that had formed in the night.

They stood there quietly with their arms around each other until the storm had passed.

Caroline raised her head and looked up at him. "Austin..."

"Shh...." He put a finger to her lips. "Don't say anything, please." He took in a shaky breath and gradually released her from his embrace. Then he felt something rubbing against his leg, and he bent over and picked up the big tomcat waiting at his feet. "It's time Jake and I were going home." His eyes came back to hers as if he couldn't bear to look away from her. "I'll call you, Caroline."

"Promise?"

"I promise." He dropped a light kiss on her mouth, turned, and with Jake under his arm, walked out into the night.

Caroline watched him go. It was some time before she remembered that she'd forgotten to tell him goodnight. She'd forgotten to tell him thank-you. She'd forgotten to tell him that she might be falling in love with him....

7

CAROLINE PUT ON her terry-cloth robe and tied the belt snugly around her waist as she walked out of the steamy bathroom. She sat down at the antique vanity table in her bedroom, pulled off her shower cap and gave her head a good shake. Long, leisurely strokes with a brush brought her hair back to life, leaving it in soft, dark waves down her back. She took a bottle of nail polish from a side drawer and set it within easy reach. She had just finished filing her fingernails when a knock sounded at her bedroom door. "Come in!" she called out.

"Hi, Mom." Jeremy strolled in and stretched out belly down on the walnut-burl bed that dominated the room. His long legs dangled over the edge of the mattress as he looked over at her. "Are you busy?"

"I was about to put a coat of polish on my nails, that's all."

He turned over and stared up at the ceiling. "Are you going out with Mr. Perry again tonight?"

"Yes, I am," she said carefully. "But I thought he gave you permission to call him Austin."

He shrugged his thin shoulders. "He did." There was adultlike scorn in his boyish voice when he added, "At least he didn't ask me to call him Uncle Austin."

And they said elephants never forgot. Actually, it was children who never forgot anything, Caroline realized as she gave the bottle of pale pink nail polish a shake. One of the few dates she'd had in the past couple of years had been an unqualified disaster from beginning to end. The man had seemed nice enough when they'd been introduced by mutual acquaintances, but he had turned out to be a real jerk. *Jerk* was Jeremy's word, not hers.

Her son had been right, of course; the man had been a jerk. For openers, he'd insisted that the boy call him "Uncle Chuck" from the moment the two met. Then Chuck had spent most of the evening complaining to Caroline about all the problems he was having with his ex-wife. Not surprisingly, there had been no second date.

Men like that were an excellent reason not to remarry, Caroline reminded herself. She'd read somewhere that it took "a mighty good husband to be better than none at all." She couldn't agree more.

She glanced over to see her son plucking at the fringe on her bedspread. "Please don't do that," she reprimanded him in a friendly but firm tone.

He looked up at her, his blue eyes hauntingly serious. At times there was a quality about her son that wasn't the least bit childlike. More than once she'd wondered if she had made him too sensitive to her feelings, to the feelings of others. After all, one day he would have to survive in a world where "men were men."

There was something on Jeremy's mind. It might take a week or even two for him to decide he was finally ready to talk about it. Then he'd just blurt it out at the most unexpected moment. That was his way.

His clear blue eyes flickered with curiosity. "Did you love my father?"

"Yes, I loved your father very much," Caroline stated, looking directly at him so he would know it was the truth.

He hadn't asked that question in a long time, a year or more at least. But she always answered it in the same way. She had no intention of keeping Jim's memory alive in any morbid sense, but Jeremy deserved to know about the man who had been his father.

There was a photograph of Jim Douglas on his son's dresser. It was an enlarged, candid snapshot of a handsome young man in his prime. A man of some twenty-eight years with brown curly hair and intelligent brown eyes. It was the photograph of a man who would never age.

Now Jeremy was coming to that age when he missed not having a father in so many ways. It was a crucial age, to Caroline's mind. She tried to do the things with her son that any father would do, but there were limits to even her capabilities.

Last summer had been a perfect illustration. She had tried to throw a baseball around with him out in the backyard. But after a few negligible attempts, Jeremy had scornfully declared that she threw the ball "like a girl," and he had gone off to find a friend to play with instead. She would never be another Mickey Mantle.

And that was the least of her problems in trying to be both mother and father to a growing boy.

Caroline had finished polishing the nails of one hand before she sensed that Jeremy was ready to talk. Emotions were difficult for an adult to articulate. How much more difficult they must be for a ten-year-old boy who was struggling between the worlds of child and adult.

"Do you like your life, Mom?" he asked quietly.

Now where had that come from, Caroline wondered in amazement. And why? She mustn't answer too quickly. Jeremy would feel she was giving him a superficial answer.

"Yes, I like my life." She paused significantly. "I like it very much. I have you—" she smiled across the room at him "—and Grandma and Grandpa to love. I have my business and my friends. I have this comfortable house to live in, and I have my health. When I stop and think about it, Jeremy, I have a great deal to be thankful for. Yes, I like my life."

"I like *my* life," he volunteered with a decisive nod. "And you know what? I like Austin, too."

Caroline was quick to suppress a smile. "Do you?"

He faced her squarely, certain of his feelings, at least in this matter. "Yes. He doesn't treat me like a little kid. I like that."

"I'm glad you like Austin, because I like him, too," she said.

"Are you gonna marry him?" Jeremy asked boldly.

So they were finally getting to the crux of the matter. This is why he'd come into her room tonight for a little chat. When Caroline gazed into those big blue eyes of his, she saw uncertainty there, and something else. Something that she couldn't quite decipher. Was it hope? The same hope she'd seen on the faces of her family and friends these past few weeks?

She straightened and briskly announced, "No, I'm not going to marry Austin Perry."

He frowned. "Why not?"

"Well, for one thing he hasn't asked me."

Jeremy never wavered. "I thought girls could ask boys that kind of stuff. I know the girls in our school ask the boys to go to movies and parties."

"Well, I don't," Caroline responded evenly. "Besides, Austin and I are just friends. Good friends."

Jeremy glanced at the clock on the mahogany end table and scooted off the edge of her bed. She was a little surprised, but that answer seemed to satisfy him. "Well, I gotta go, Mom. That karate movie is on TV in five minutes, and Grandpa is going to watch it with me. Grandma said she'd make some popcorn for us."

"Enjoy your show!" she called after him as his lithe form disappeared out the bedroom door.

Caroline shook her head as she finished applying polish to her nails. Afterward she remained seated at her vanity table, staring thoughtfully into space.

Before Jeremy had been born, she'd never suspected how deep the maternal instinct would flow in her. It seemed to grow as Jeremy himself grew. And then when Jim had been killed, she'd clung to their son as though he were her lifeline. No longer a wife, she dedicated herself to being a mother.

Was there a love greater than that of mother for child? She thought not. It reached down to the very center, to the very heart, of a woman and changed her forever. All the frustrations and the tears, the bone-weariness and the worries—all of that couldn't change the abiding love of a mother for her child. Body of her body. Heart of her heart. Jeremy was her heart.

But her son was growing up, changing, becoming a mystery to her in many ways. There was an age-old gulf that always came between male and female, even between mother and son.

He was going to be eleven in several months, and all the signs were there: the legs that seemed to go on forever, the boy's body poised on the brink of puberty, a growing—if surreptitious—interest in girls. He had confided to her only last week that he had a girlfriend. A cute little blonde with a ponytail who was in his reading group at school. And he'd asked her to buy deodorant for him at the grocery store. Now he spent more time brushing his teeth and combing his hair than Caroline did.

Caroline laughed quietly to herself as she took her bathrobe off and began to get dressed for her date with Austin. To think of all the times in the past couple of years that she'd had to be after Jeremy to wash his face, brush his teeth, clean the grime out from under his fingernails. The times were changing, and it was all going too fast, this childhood of her Jeremy's.

What had she been like in the fifth grade? Caroline searched her mind for some remembrance of that girl of long ago. A little girl in French braids and a pink dress. Girls didn't wear jeans in those days. And she'd had a boyfriend. She could still remember his name. Dennis. Perhaps things really hadn't changed that much, after all.

She glanced at the alarm clock on the bedside table; she'd better hurry if she wanted to be ready when Austin showed up at the door. After more than a month and some half-dozen dates to the movies, out to dinner and to concerts at the Denver Center for the Performing Arts, the man was finally inviting her to his home. For dinner, no less. She wouldn't be honest with herself if she didn't admit that the prospect of spending an evening alone with him filled her with some trepidation. There had always been people around on the other occasions, and consequently, physical intimacy had been kept to a minimum.

And it was just as well, Caroline thought, slipping her dress over her head and smoothing its chic lines down her hips. Things had a tendency to move too fast between Austin and her as it was.

She'd bought this bright yellow crinkled cotton dress only yesterday. It had cap sleeves and a nipped-in waist. The gored skirt had yards and yards of material that flared around her long legs. It wasn't the most expensive dress she'd ever owned, but it was quickly becoming one of her favorites.

She reached behind her with both hands, found the tab on the zipper and eased it up her back. Her feet slid into high-heeled sandals that matched her straw handbag. The final touches were a spray, here on the back of her wrist and there at her nape, of her favorite perfume. The only pieces of jewelry she wore were her gold watch and a pair of small pearl earrings.

She did a small pirouette in front of the full-length mirror. Yes, yellow was definitely her color, she told herself wryly. Coward that she was!

"Well, on that confident note..." she muttered as she made her way downstairs.

She had scarcely sat on the sofa beside Jeremy when the doorbell rang. Austin was standing on her doorstep in an elegant blue suede blazer and charcoal-gray slacks.

He was beautiful.

There was no other way of describing the man. The lapis blue of his jacket accentuated the endless blue depths of his eyes. He was tall and lean and muscular and inviting.

"Hello, Caroline," he said, stepping into the hallway and stopping to kiss her. His mouth lingered unexpectedly on hers. He hadn't kissed her like that in weeks. It left her feeling a bit weak in the knees. "Let me say a quick hello and an even quicker goodbye to your family. Then let's get out of here," he urged in a husky voice as he drew back.

Yet his greetings to her family were both polite and friendly. He seemed to know just the right things to say and do: commenting on the lovely color of Edna's new sweater; bringing along a volume on Colorado's history in case Harry would like to read it, as well as a large nugget of iron pyrite, fool's gold, for Jeremy's rock collection. With that irresistible charm of his, he had them all eating out of the palm of his hand.

Caroline heard her own voice sounding slightly distorted, as if it were coming from a great distance, as she said, "Good night, Mother and Dad." She leaned over, dropped a kiss on the top of Jeremy's head and admonished lightly, "Be sure you get to bed right after the movie is over."

Then she was helped into her raincoat, and they went out into the May night. A night of dark trees and gray, cloudy skies, the streetlight on the corner silvery in the clinging mist.

Austin gallantly handed her into his car. Caroline sank down into the posh interior of the Cadillac. She enjoyed the smell and the feel of the fine leather and the promise of power that lay beneath the soft purr of the engine as he maneuvered the sleek black Eldorado through the streets of Denver. She sat back and luxuriated in the special magic of the misty spring night. The soft, sensuous music of a local FM station emanated from the car radio.

The next thing she knew, Austin was pulling into his driveway, and, just before he drove into the garage, she could see his house illuminated by remote-controlled spotlights. The house was cantilevered glass and stone that clung to a mountainside on the outskirts of the metropolitan area. It was contemporary and low to the ground and not at all reminiscent of his rustic log cabin high in the mountains.

"Welcome to my home," Austin said as he escorted her inside.

Caroline stood in the dimly lit front room and looked out on the muted lights of the city below. "It's beautiful up here," she said in hushed tones.

"Yes, it is. Let me show you around before we have a drink." He took her coat. "This house was designed and built by an architect who was a confirmed bachelor," he explained.

She could see what he meant. The house had only three rooms. One large bedroom with a very large bed, a compact kitchen with all the latest technological gadgets and equipment, and an expansive front room that served as an entertainment center, the living room, the games room and even the dining room, all in one. There was a mammoth, double-sided stone fireplace, open on one side to the room in which they stood; on the other side it opened into the bedroom.

Austin's home was luxurious. It was expensive. It was masculine. It was a bachelor's paradise, Caroline realized as they concluded their tour of the house.

"What would you like to drink?" Austin inquired as he left her side and strolled over to the wet bar nestled in one corner of the room.

She tried to think of something simple. "I was going to say whatever you're having," she said, smiling at him a little uneasily. "Then I remembered that you usually drink Scotch on the rocks." With a grimace she added, "So I'll have a glass of wine, please."

"Would you prefer white or red?"

Caroline shrugged. "Whichever is handy will do, thank you." Waiting for him to bring her drink, she looked around the room with its modern art and its U-shaped sectional sofa in chrome and leather that must seat at least a dozen people. Between the fireplace and the windows opposite it, there was an intimate table set for two. She turned and watched Austin's reflection in the wall of glass as he poured her sparkling white wine and came across the room to hand it to her.

"Thank you," she murmured as she turned back to gaze out the window. The lights of the city below seemed to twinkle like the lights on a Christmas tree.

Caroline watched as Austin lit the logs in the fireplace before fixing himself a drink and leaving it on the bar. He disappeared into the kitchen for a moment and returned with a party tray in each hand, setting them on a buffet table between the sofa and where she was standing. She was still watching their reflections when Austin sauntered up to stand beside her, drink in hand.

"Would you like some chilled shrimp or pork pâté?"

Caroline raised an eyebrow and gazed up at him. "Don't tell me—your favorite delicatessen again, right?"

"Wrong." He named one of the finer restaurants in the area.

Later as they sat down to a dinner of beef tenderloin with horseradish whip, served with tender artichoke hearts holding a light, fluffy sauce, he confessed, "I wish I could tell you I was a gourmet cook, but the truth is the restaurant did the entrée, too."

"I think I can find it in my heart to forgive you," she said magnanimously as she raised the first delectable morsel to her mouth.

"You better eat up, then," Austin urged. "Jake's waiting in the kitchen for any leftovers, and he's particularly fond of beef tenderloin. Have you had a busy week?" he went on in a conversational tone.

Caroline's eyes widened appreciably over the rim of her crystal wineglass. "Every week is a busy week right now," she told him as she set the glass down on the linen tablecloth. "This is one of the most hectic times of the year in my business, but it's also one of the most exciting. We're scouting the entire country for antique ornaments and decorations or new handmade ones commissioned from craftsmen. One of my buyers came back this week with a collection of country dolls she'd found in Wisconsin while she was visiting her parents. We know they were all hand painted by the same person around 1870. It was a very exciting find. And one of the dealers I keep in close touch with recently led me to a man who wanted to sell his collection of antique cast-iron toys."

"Cast-iron toys?" Austin repeated incredulously. "Is there much money to be made in selling old toys as holiday decorations?"

"Yes, there is. If you haven't checked your attic recently, you might want to. There was a series of rare toys made by the Hubley Manufacturing Company in Lancaster, Pennsylvania, from 1919 to 1926. They were called Royal Circus. One horse-drawn circus wagon, sixteen inches long, recently sold at Sotheby's for a record nineteen thousand dollars plus."

He gave a low, appreciative whistle. "I had no idea old toys were in that kind of demand."

"You and a lot of other people. Someone could have a fortune sitting in their attic, and they wouldn't even know it. I feel it's my job to let them know," Caroline said, smiling beneficently.

"I didn't realize you had to be a detective in your line of work," Austin commented, taking another bite of beef tenderloin.

"Discovering a rare old ornament or a decoration or a new artisan is my favorite part of the business," she admitted, her cheeks glowing in her excitement. "That and the fact that, in my business, it's Christmas in April and May as well as in December."

"It must be a little like celebrating Christmas all year round," he said, smiling. "How many people do you have out scouring the countryside for buried treasure?"

"I have a permanent staff of ten people here in Denver. That includes office personnel and buyers. Of course, there are dozens of craftsmen and artists working for me on commission."

"And all of this started with your hobby of . . ." He rubbed his chin thoughtfully. "Working with wax figures, right?"

"Right. I made miniature figurines in antique molds to begin with. I'll show you sometime. I still make a few wax figures every year during the holiday season." She smiled reminiscently. "It's a reminder of what my roots are, so to speak."

"Sometime I'd like to see what you do," he said with evident interest, then offered her a choice from the bread basket. "Let's see, we have a braided bread made of Edam cheese, lemon peel and cardamom, topped with a sprinkle of sugar." He was reciting as if he'd memorized the ingredients. "Or there's a honey and poppy seed brioche, if you prefer the traditional French roll."

"They both look delicious," Caroline said as she accepted one of the rolls.

"You can take the rest home for your family, if you'd like," Austin said generously. "How long will your parents be living with you, by the way?" he inquired with the same nonchalance usually reserved for a discussion of the weather.

Much as he liked Edna and Harry Davis, a man could hardly attempt a serious love affair with a woman in a house full of people. And Austin had made up his mind that a serious relationship was what he wanted. In fact, he intended to apply the same basic principles to his seduction of Caroline Douglas that had made him the successful businessman he was today: define your goals and then go after what you want with single-minded determination. Frankly, he preferred that the Davises be out of the way.

"Mother and Dad were up at their condominium most of this week overseeing the selection of new carpeting and wallpaper and paint. You remember that I told you they're redecorating? Well, they hope to be moved back in no later than the Fourth of July. They'll stay in Colorado through the summer. Then they always arrange to fly back to Florida in the fall." Caroline paused as she broke the light, rich roll in two. "They spend less than half the year here, you know. My parents don't usually camp on my doorstep like they have been this past month. In fact, they changed their schedule this spring and flew back several months early to supervise the remodeling of their condominium."

All the while she was talking, Austin was groaning to himself. The Fourth of July! That was still weeks away. Heaven knows, he was a patient man. Hadn't he proved that this past month? But another six or seven weeks. Patience be hanged!

He helped himself to another slice of beef tenderloin and ate half of it before he could think of something to say. "Harry has told me on several occasions that he doesn't regret taking early retirement."

Caroline nodded. "No, and neither does my mother. Dad was ready to retire three years ago when he turned sixty-two. Perhaps he'd looked at his own statistics as an insurance-company executive and decided to beat the actuary tables." She laughed a little. "I think they're busier now than they were before they retired. Of course, they both love to ski and golf and swim and travel. They have the best of both worlds by maintaining a home here and in Florida."

"I wish Gus felt that way about his retirement," his son said feelingly.

"Perhaps he would have if your mother had lived. Being alone at his age must make all the difference, you know," she pointed out sympathetically.

"I guess you're right," Austin conceded, putting his fork down. Then he turned his head and gazed out at the lights of the city below. "Denver sure sparkles from up here, doesn't she?"

"Yes, just like a silver lady." Caroline sighed. "You have the most magnificent view of the city I've ever seen."

Austin seemed preoccupied for a moment, finally muttering under his breath, "Hell hath no fury like a Silver Lady scorned."

"Is that a line from a poem or something?"

"It's from the latest nuisance letter I've received," he told her as he picked up his fork again.

"You got another threatening letter?"

Austin scowled. "If you want to call it that. It contained only that one line about the Silver Lady. Not much of a threat in my book." He pushed an artichoke around on his plate.

"The Silver Lady is a mine you're closing, isn't she?"

"One of several silver mines we're closing down, as a matter of fact."

"Have you notified the police?" She seemed more concerned about the incident than he was.

"No. But I did turn the note over to the company's security division. They couldn't make any more of it than I had. Someone is unhappy, and this is their way of letting me know about it." He seemed to lose interest in talking about the anonymous letter. "Tell me, how's Jeremy doing these days?"

It was obvious he wanted to change the subject. Caroline decided to go along with him. "He's been a little antsy lately. I think he's ready for school to be out for the summer."

Austin nodded. "He's a good kid. You've done a heck of a job raising him all by yourself, Caroline."

"Thank you. I think he's a good kid, too."

Austin polished off his dinner and pushed his plate away as if the action had some special significance. He took a drink of water and cleared his throat. "I've become quite fond of Edna and Harry and especially of Jeremy during the past month," he said, setting his glass down.

Caroline placed her knife and fork on her dinner plate and confided with a smile, "They all adore you."

He reached across the table and took her hand in his, drawing it toward him. He brought her fingertips to his lips. "And you? Do you adore me, too, Caroline?"

She could feel her name vibrating on his lips, and little slivers of awareness darted along her skin and up her arm. He was asking her if she adored him. Yet he was asking far more than that. He knew that as surely as she did.

"Of course I adore you." She laughed self-consciously. "We all adore you, Austin." She drew her hand back, then placed the linen napkin beside her plate and announced in a slightly nervous voice, "Now let's clear away the leftover food and dirty dishes, shall we?"

She was only delaying the inevitable. Caroline admitted as much to herself as she picked up her dinner plate and got to her feet. Austin Perry wanted her. That was clear enough. And she wanted him. She could weep for wanting him—she had. But she was a coward. She was afraid. Afraid that she had forgotten all she had ever known of men, of love, of sex. Afraid to let physical passion rule her actions. That kind of passion might be forgivable at twenty or even at twenty-five, but it wasn't at her age. Everything she did now affected other people, as well. She couldn't rush into a love affair with this man. She mustn't. There was too much at stake.

"All right," he agreed at last. "We'll clean up first."

"I'll wash the dishes if you want to put the food away and take care of the table."

"Then we'll have Irish coffee in front of the fire," Austin suggested.

"That sounds delightful," she called back over her shoulder as she disappeared into the kitchen.

A half hour later they were sitting on the soft leather sofa in front of the fire, sipping their Irish coffee. The soft glow of the firelight, the intimacy of the late hour, the sensuous mood weaving its inevitable spell, the knowledge that they were alone together at last. It was all there in the night air surrounding them.

"This has been a lovely ending to a lovely dinner," Caroline said as she balanced the porcelain mug in her hand.

"It seemed like a good idea on a cool evening like this," Austin agreed, moving a little closer to her. Then he chuckled, the sound low and deep from the back of his throat.

"What's so amusing?" she asked, suspicious of his sudden jovial mood.

"You've got a dab of whipped cream on your lip. No, let me," he said softly, seductively, as he leaned toward her and licked the confection from her mouth.

Caroline could feel herself quiver as he continued along her upper lip and down around to the lower one with excruciatingly slow movements. He paused at the tiny juncture at the corner of her mouth and flicked the tip of his tongue over the sensitive skin. She could feel her lips beginning to open to him as the petals of a flower open to the sun, turning toward the source of their light and warmth.

"Careful," Austin warned with a husky growl as he took the coffee mug from her hand and set it on the buffet table behind them. "We don't want you spilling hot coffee on me. I do it well enough all by myself, if you recall." Then he undid the knot at his throat and pulled the silk tie from around his neck. "I think I'll be more comfortable if I take this off." He undid the first two buttons of his shirt, as well. "There. That's much better. Now where were we?" he asked rhetorically, taking her into his arms again.

Caroline found herself stroking the soft material of his suede jacket. "I don't know if this is a very good idea, Austin." She knew he could hear the uncertainty in her voice.

"Well, I *do* know," he stated unswervingly. "This happens to be an excellent idea."

She trembled against him. "I'm not so sure about that."

"Let me be sure for both of us," he murmured enticingly. "Trust me, Caroline. I wouldn't do anything to hurt you. You believe that, don't you?"

"Yes, I believe you, but—"

Then his mouth descended on hers, and any further opportunity for discussion was lost. Lord, what this man could do to her with just his kiss! When he kissed her, Caroline thought vaguely, she didn't seem to have the sense she was born with. She was that quickly addicted to the feel, the taste, the touch, of his mouth. He was coaxing and cajoling a response from her one minute and fiercely demanding it the next. He gave to her, and he took away. He was so gentle that it brought tears to her eyes. Yet he could destroy her and then bring her back to life with the sweet, aching need in his kiss.

Austin tore his mouth from hers only long enough to demand the assurance he apparently needed to hear from her, "Do you want me to kiss you, Caroline?"

"Yes! Oh, yes, Austin, I want you to kiss me!" She capitulated, crying his name softly in the night. "And I want to kiss you, but—"

"But what?" he said as his mouth hovered above hers. She could feel the heat of his breath wafting over her face.

The words tumbled from her mouth. "Sometimes you frighten me, Austin. And sometimes..." She couldn't go on. She couldn't tell him. She had neither the words nor the courage to say them.

"Sometimes what?" he prompted. "We're both adults. We should be able to tell each other what we're thinking, what we're feeling."

She spoke hurriedly before she lost her nerve. "All right, then. Sometimes all I can think about is you, Austin Perry. And I don't know what to do about it." Her voice ended on an embarrassed whisper. Then there was nothing between them but silence.

Austin closed his eyes. When he opened them again, Caroline saw something in their blue depths that she'd never expected to see. It was the reflection of her own pain, her own uncertainty.

"My God, woman, I thought you knew," he murmured roughly. "I haven't stopped thinking about you since the moment we met. Don't you know that I want you more than I've ever wanted anything on the face of this earth?"

She was stunned. "You can't mean that."

"I can, and I do." He took her face in his hands and looked into her eyes for long minutes. "I want you, Caroline Douglas. I want you so much that it tears my guts apart just to think about it. I've wanted to make love to you since that first night in my cabin, and I don't know what to do about it."

Caroline tried to control herself, but it was happening to her again. All her best intentions were flying out the window in the face of his overwhelming passion for her and hers for him. She knew her head should rule her heart and not the other way around, but she was, after all, only human.

"I want to make love with you now, here, tonight," Austin declared, his mouth playing over hers, warm and welcoming.

Caroline knew he would stop if she asked him to. They both knew she wouldn't ask. But, dear Lord, she needed time to think, and there was no more time! He was waiting for her to say the words.

They started out awkwardly at first, one word stumbling over the next. Then they came more and more rapidly until she was out of breath. "I want you, Austin Perry, as I've never wanted any man. I want you. I want your touch, your kiss, your body next to mine now, here, tonight."

He stood up and held his hand out to her. Caroline rose to her feet beside him and placed her hand trustingly in his. She threaded her fingers through his fingers and squeezed tightly. Courage. That was what she must have now.

"It will be like the first time for you and for me," Austin promised her as he led the way into his bedroom. He stopped in the middle of the room and placed his hands on her shoulders. "If you're afraid, I'll understand," he rasped as he lowered his head and found her mouth with his. It was a shattering moment as he allowed her to feel just how much he cherished her, how much he desired her, how much he wanted her. "I will try to be gentle with you, my darling Caroline," he went on as he pulled away from her for an instant. "But there are limits to a man's self-control. You must know that."

"I do know. And to mine, too," she breathed into his mouth.

Austin placed his hands on her, beginning to shape her face and the silky length of her neck. He outlined her body through the dress: the inviting swell of her breasts; the firmness of her flat abdomen; the sensitive pubic bone; the soft, womanly mound that dipped between her legs. Then he started again, this time at her nape, and worked his way down her back, lingering over the small valley at the base of her spine, the curve of her hips, the rounded enticement of her derrière.

"Dear God, but you are sweet," he moaned as he fit her body to his own.

Caroline wanted to believe him. She needed to believe him. She watched as he took a half step away and shrugged off his jacket. He tossed it over a chair behind him, then came back to her, his mouth on the curve of her neck, his teeth nipping the lobe of her ear, his hands finding the zipper down the back of her dress. He eased the material off her shoulders. She quickly stepped out of her dress and shoes.

"Let me see you, sweetheart. Let me see you by the glow of the fire's light," he urged as he held her at arm's length. His gaze swept over her from the lacy bodice of her slip to the silky line of her hip and down the long, lovely length of her legs.

Caroline's hands reached out for Austin, unbuttoning his dress shirt and helping him to take it off. He pulled his T-shirt over his head in one well-executed motion, and he was left bare to the waist. His hair was crisp and his skin golden by the firelight. His torso was firm and muscular. This was the way she always imagined him. This was the way she saw him in her dreams.

Her hands went to him as if of their own volition. Her first caress was hesitant, tentative, exploratory. When she discovered that her slightest touch made him quiver in his shoes, it gave her a sense of power she had never known before. It gave her the confidence she needed to go on. She believed that her desire to please him was the only thing that made up for her lack of recent experience. Sex was something Caroline remembered every now and then as if in a dream. Sex had no reality for her. It had no meaning for her. Except for the reality and the meaning this man promised to give to it.

They finished undressing by the glow of the fire; it bathed the bed in front of it in soft light and left shadows in the far corners of the room. Caroline took a long time arranging her dress and slip and panty hose over a chair before turning back to Austin, uncertain if she should slip out of the lacy bits of her bra and panties.

He was standing there naked. There was a sinewy strength to his long legs and lean thighs that was in perfect harmony with his muscular arms and broad chest. The taut lines of his abdomen emphasized the cloud of crisp, curling hair that arrowed down his body to disappear into the shadows.

"You're beautiful," she whispered.

Then she saw the wonder of his manhood. It was proud and powerful, and it fascinated her. She lost most of her inhibitions even as she stood there studying his body, wanting to reach out, to touch, to caress, to grasp, to feel the tempered steel in its velvety sheath.

Austin made no move toward her. He simply stood and allowed her to look. Caroline took a step toward him, and immediately she could see that her action pleased him. Some barely perceptible change in the color of his eyes and in the slant of his head told her so. Then she reached out and gently enfolded him in her grasp. Her name was on his lips that quickly.

"Caroline!"

He seemed incapable of speaking for several minutes as she allowed her hands to roam over the muscular planes of his thighs, his abdomen, his chest, his arms, his shoulders. Everywhere she touched him, she gave pleasure to him and received pleasure in return.

"You have to stop touching me," Austin told her with a sharp sigh. "I love what you do to me, but I can't take much more. Now it's your turn. You have to learn to receive pleasure as well as to give it."

He reached behind her and unhooked the lacy bra. He slipped the straps down her arms and caught her breasts in his hands. His first instinct was to consume her alive, to plunge that rosy peak into his mouth like a bit of fresh fruit ripe for the picking, to savor the taste of its natural sweetness. Instead, he tempered his impulse and caught the tip of one breast between his thumb and finger and squeezed gently.

Caroline's breath started to come hard and fast as her body responded to his touch. Her breasts swelled in his hands. The nipples tightened into two hard buds that would surely bloom for him in the end. She swayed on her feet from the dizzying effect of his caress and her wholehearted response to it. He caught her with one arm and pulled the bedspread back with the other. Then he settled her in the middle of the big bed and knelt over her. He kissed her deeply, completely, his tongue burrowing into her mouth. He mined the rich vein he found there, taking from her all the silver dew and golden honey within.

Then he blazed a path along her flesh. She arched instinctively, and he captured her breast in his mouth and sucked at its enticing tip until his name became a litany on her lips. He left a trail of fire down her body. Her skin was sensitive to his slightest touch, to the merest whisper of a kiss as he drew the last bit of lace from her body.

Austin let his weight press her into the mattress, and she was literally, physically, overpowered by him. He defined the parameters of her world. The fathomless depths of his eyes were as infinite and immense as the night skies. His shoulders were as solid and as honest as the earth itself. His kiss sank oceans deep, drowning her, reviving her, only to drown her again in the next wave, the next sensual assault.

Caroline felt a tantalizing tension building within her as he rolled onto his side, taking her with him, his hands grasping her buttocks, his nails lightly scoring her tender flesh. Then he found that small, vulnerable bud with the tip of his finger, and her response was both immediate and overwhelming. Like a piece of fine crystal, she felt herself shattering into a thousand tiny shards.

"Austin, please! I know that I said I wouldn't be afraid, but I am. I am afraid!" she gasped, digging her fingernails into his shoulders.

"You have nothing to be afraid of, Caroline," he assured her in a husky voice as he gathered her nearer to him. "Hold on to me, darling. You have nothing to fear as long as I'm with you. I've waited so long for you. We'll be so good together. I promise."

He stroked her gently then, soothing her with his kiss and with his touch. And when she was no longer afraid, he found her again with his fingertip, moving in the merest hint of a caress. A soft, feminine sound came from the back of her throat as he delved gently within, and then he probed deeper and deeper until all fear was dissolved, swept aside by a wondrous feeling she had never known before, never imagined in her wildest dreams, waking or sleeping.

"I want you, Austin! I want you now!" Caroline heard herself chant as she reached out for him, urging him closer.

Moving above her, he bent over her and parted her legs with his own, finding the secret core of her just as the miner burrows deeply into the earth to find its core of riches.

"I've waited for you so long, Caroline," he breathed. "I can't wait any longer, sweetheart!"

Then he was there between her thighs, probing gently at first, finding her warm and willing and inviting. He thrilled to the knowledge that she trembled in his arms even as he moved to alleviate the strange ache in his body. He felt her close around him like a velvet glove, and he drove deeper. His flesh was throbbing with need, and only this woman could bring him the sweet relief he sought.

Caroline felt her mind and body hovering on the brink for one precious moment before Austin thrust into her again and sent her over the edge. She was drowning. She was flying. She had no breath left in her body. There was nothing to her but this raging hunger, this desire, this need for the man whose hunger and desire and need were as great as her own.

And then that sublime tension was building again, this time to a feverish pitch. She clung to him for dear life, not daring to let go even for an instant. She cried out as she soared into the blue, so blue sky. She floated far above the clouds, nearly touching the heavens themselves. Or was she only lost in his eyes?

"Caroline! My sweet Caroline!" His hoarse cry echoed her flight into ecstasy.

She felt him shudder again and again as he called her name. They held on to each other in the aftershock, clinging to each other. For that too-brief moment of time, they thought, they felt that they were as one.

Caroline opened her eyes later, much later, and there was the moonlight, the firelight, the love-light in Austin's eyes. If she was to die now, she mused as if in a waking dream, at least there would be no regrets when it came to this: she had loved and been loved by the best of men.

Austin stretched out beside her on the bed and wrapped his arms around her. He murmured close to her ear, "I told you we'd be good together."

She put her head back over the crook of his arm and gazed up at him with eyes still clouded from their love-making. He looked very pleased with himself, she thought. "Yes, we were good together," she said contentedly as she snuggled into his side.

"We were great together!" Austin crowed as he wadded one of the king-size pillows beneath his head.

Later, after staring up at the ceiling for an inordinate amount of time, he said, "Caroline, I've been thinking . . ."

"Yes?" she murmured drowsily.

He turned his head and looked down at her. "I've been thinking that we should consider a merger."

She wrinkled her brow. "A merger? You want to buy me out?"

He pulled her a little closer to him. "No, I don't want to buy you out. I want to marry you."

"Marry me?" Her voice broke off on the last word. She took a deep breath and tried again. "What are you talking about?" she asked, propping herself up on one elbow.

"I'm talking about getting married. You and me. I'll have to sell this place, of course. It was fine for a bachelor, but it's hardly suitable for a family. I suppose I could move into your place, or we could go shopping for a new house altogether."

For a moment Caroline felt as though she was trapped in the fun house at the carnival. The kind filled with mirrors that distorted reality into grotesque shapes and sizes. Her head was spinning, her mind reeling with the realization that this man assumed, now that they'd made love, that he was going to take charge of her life—just like that. Just as he had taken charge of her car that day it had died in the snow. Well, he had another think coming. It was time Austin Perry was told a few facts of life.

Caroline pulled the sheet up around her shoulders. "I've been married," she began.

"Not to me, you haven't," he shot back.

Obviously a more direct approach was needed. "I'm not sure I want to get married again," she told him firmly.

His blue eyes narrowed slightly. "Are you telling me that you won't marry me?"

"I didn't say that." Obviously the direct approach had its shortcomings. Caroline took a deep breath and tried again. "You've got to understand, Austin. I'm not the type of woman who likes to rush into things, into anything. Why, it can take me a week or two just to decide on a new dress or a new pair of shoes."

"Then you obviously need someone who's decisive. And there is no one more decisive than I am."

She frowned. "That's part of what's worrying me. You are a decisive man. You seem to know exactly what you want. I'm not as sure of what I want. This whole thing between us has gone too fast for me. It—it makes me nervous. I don't even know for sure how I ended up in your bed tonight."

Austin smiled. "Would you like me to demonstrate?"

She swallowed. "No, I just want you to understand. I need some time."

"Time for what?" he complained impatiently.

She smiled at him. "It's not an unreasonable request, you know."

He folded his arms across his chest. "I'm not feeling very reasonable at the moment. How much time will you need?"

"I don't know. I need some time to think things over. Time to consider the pros and cons. Time to get to know you better. If I marry at this point in my life, I have to think of more than just my own feelings." She grabbed on to anything she could to support her argument. "There's Jeremy to think of, and I haven't even met your family yet."

He arched a dark brow in her direction. "Jeremy and I get along just fine. But you mean you want to meet Gus and Charlie?"

"Of course I want to meet your father and your uncle. They're your family, aren't they?"

He nodded. "All right. When?"

It seemed he was going to pin her down right there and then. "How about sometime in the next week or two?" Caroline suggested.

"Shall we say for lunch this Thursday?"

"I suppose I could make it for lunch this week. I'll need to check my calendar at the office, of course."

"Lunch on Thursday it is, then. I'll call you on Monday to make sure you have that day open."

"That will be fine," she agreed, nervously fingering the edge of the sheet. "I'm not making any promises. You have to understand that, Austin. This decision is too important for you to try to hurry me."

He looked at her, brooding. "I understand. I don't like it, but I do understand."

Caroline glanced over at the clock on the bedside table. "It's getting awfully late. I should get dressed and be on my way home."

He dragged her closer and told her in a husky voice, "Later. I'll take you home later, darling." He lowered his head and found her mouth.

"Yes, later," Caroline murmured as she wrapped her arms tightly around him.

8

THE WOMAN WAS SOMETHING of a paradox, Austin Perry concluded as he watched her walk across the hotel lobby toward him. But then, what woman wasn't?

Caroline looked good today. Really good. She was starting to look that way to him most of the time. Hell, *all* of the time, he had to admit.

She was wearing a neat little summer suit that skimmed her thighs and clung rather nicely to the curve of her derrière. He didn't know what kind of material it was, but he noticed how well the suit fit her before he realized that that particular shade of red complemented the chestnut brown of her hair.

She raised her hand in greeting and gave him a quick smile when she was still halfway across the lobby. He could see there was a pinkish glow to her cheeks, as though she were rushing to meet him. At least that was the image of her that he preferred to carry around in his head.

One of the images, he corrected himself. The other was far more personal and private.

Austin groaned to himself as he felt his groin tighten with the recent, familiar stirrings of semiarousal. Who would have thought that the Grand Passion of his life would show up now, when he was thirty-eight, when most unmarried men assumed the rest of their lives would be spent in one lukewarm affair or another, with no strings attached? That went to show a man should never get too cocky. Life and its little ironies were always there to trip him up when he least expected it.

Yes, the joke was definitely on him this time. Just when he'd concluded that he didn't know what he was looking for in a woman, the right woman had literally landed on his doorstep. And Caroline Douglas was the right woman for him, just as he was the right man for her, even if she didn't know it yet.

Austin shook his head, contemplating what could be the major stumbling block to the success of his plans. Maybe it wasn't so much that Caroline didn't know he was the right man for her; maybe she was simply afraid to admit it.

She was a paradox, that was for sure. She talked about being a coward, and she was a terrible coward about the craziest little things. But she was also one of the bravest human beings he'd ever met. She had started out with nothing and built herself a small empire in less than seven years. In a split second of tragic carelessness on someone else's part, she had been left on her own to raise a small child, and she had done a great job with Jeremy. Being both mother and father to a growing boy in today's world took courage, if anything did.

She admitted to being a cautious woman who could take forever to decide on something as inconsequential as a pair of shoes—and then she made love with him and held nothing of herself back. In bed, she was totally without pretension. She gave as good as she got.

Sweet as an angel one moment, a wildly passionate woman the next.

And she needed him as much as he needed her, Austin decided as she came closer. He could see that plainly enough. Why couldn't she? Maybe it was that damned list! That list of requirements she thought she had to have in a man. What mortal could hope to live up to that idealized hero she'd conjured up in her head over the years? Hero or not, he was the man for her. Of that much he was sure.

Whatever state of indecision Caroline was in, he'd never felt better in his life than he had since they'd made love last weekend. In the past few days he had come to realize that everything he'd ever wanted in life was now within his grasp. Almost. He still had to find a way to make Caroline see that they were meant for each other.

Easier said than done, Austin acknowledged as he started toward her.

Caroline glanced down at her wristwatch. She was a good ten minutes early. She had assumed she would be the first to arrive at the hotel restaurant Austin had chosen for their lunch with his father and uncle. But here he was coming toward her now, looking every bit as attractive and certainly every bit as overwhelming as she'd remembered. Seeing him like this, for the first time since they'd made love, brought such a sweet rush of feeling that she nearly ran the last two steps into his arms. But propriety and the public setting forbade that indiscretion. Instead, they took one final step toward each other and stopped.

Austin was the first to speak. "Hello, Caroline," he murmured in a deep voice as he bent over and kissed her on the cheek, his lips skimming the corner of her mouth.

She nearly turned her head and offered him more, but common sense won out, and she responded in kind, "Hello, Austin. You're even earlier than I am. I thought I'd be the first one here."

"I had a meeting in this part of town this morning. We wrapped it up sooner than I thought. And I wanted to make sure I was here before Gus and Charlie arrived. I wasn't about to leave you to their less-than-tender mercies."

"You make them sound like a couple of old ogres." She laughed uncertainly.

"Not ogres, but they aren't two completely harmless old men, either." He said this as if it were his duty to warn her.

"Now you are making me nervous." She took her compact from her handbag long enough to quickly check her hair and makeup.

"Don't worry, you look beautiful," Austin assured her in a voice turned slightly husky. "And I didn't mean to make Gus and Charlie sound like anything more or less than they are."

"And what's that?" she asked, putting the compact back in her purse and snapping the clasp shut.

He seemed to be searching for the right words. "I guess you could say they're just a couple of eccentric old coots who, at the worst, will bend your ear with their endless stories and reminiscences about the 'good old days.'"

Caroline put a reassuring hand on his arm and smiled up at him. "I won't mind too much if they bend my ear. We all like to reminisce sometimes. Especially as we get older and the past seems so much more inviting than the future."

Austin gazed down at her with genuine affection. "You're really a very sweet woman, do you know that?" he said, looking as though he might kiss her right then and there.

She felt warmth spreading over her face. "I'm not sure I should take that as a compliment."

"Believe me, it was meant as one," he stated categorically. He glanced at his watch. "It's still early. Why don't we find a place to sit down until Gus and Charlie show up?"

"There are several comfortable-looking armchairs over by that pillar. We should be able to see the front door and most of the hotel lobby from there."

Austin smiled at her and slipped his arm through hers. "We better grab them quick before someone else takes them."

After they were settled, Caroline thought to ask, "By the way, have you received any more of those anonymous letters?"

Austin shrugged his broad shoulders. "No. No more telephone calls. No more anonymous letters. Nothing. My guess is whoever it was simply gave up. They probably realized that you can't stand in the way of progress."

"Yes, we wouldn't want to get in the way of progress, now, would we?" she said with just the slightest trace of sarcasm in her voice.

"Hey, whose side are you on, anyway?" Austin teased.

Caroline relented a little but still pointed out, "I wasn't aware of the fact that I had to choose sides."

"Well, *I* choose for you to be on my side," he said with a glint of satisfaction in his eye. "By the way, there's something I may have forgotten to mention to you about my father and my uncle."

Caroline's eyes widened as she exclaimed, "They're twins, aren't they?"

Austin was visibly amazed. "Yes, but how did you guess?"

"Because two older gentlemen just walked into the lobby of the hotel. They're obviously twins, and they're headed straight for us. Therefore, the odds are fairly good that the two men are your father and your uncle."

Austin gave a low, appreciative whistle. "I am impressed." Then he added, "If you ever decide to give up the Christmas-designs business, you'd make a hell of a detective, lady." He turned to watch the two older men. "Actually, they used to look more alike than they do now. Charlie has put on some weight, especially around the middle, and Gus has lost more of his hair. He's mortified about that, too, since he's the younger of the two."

Caroline nodded sympathetically. "Since they're identical twins, he couldn't be the younger by much."

"He's not. Ten, maybe fifteen minutes. I used to know exactly. They'll tell you the whole story if you make the mistake of asking them," he said, giving her ample warning. "Oh-oh. I see they're stopping at the hotel drugstore before joining us. That could only mean one thing."

She had to ask, of course. "What?"

"Cigars."

Caroline wrinkled her forehead. "Cigars?"

Austin nodded. "They're buying cigars to smoke after lunch. If the smoke bothers you, don't hesitate to speak up. The air can get pretty thick sometimes with the two of them puffing away like a couple of chimneys."

"If I start choking, I'll be sure to let you know," Caroline said dryly. She suddenly realized she was drawing random circles on the arm of the chair with her fingernail. She folded her hands in her lap and wondered aloud, "I've read about the unusual closeness that exists between twins—mentally, physically, even spiritually. It must have been—" she searched for a discreet word "—different having a father who was half of a set of identical twins."

Austin mulled that over for a minute before responding. "Yes, it was different. Right from the start Mother had to get used to the idea that Charlie was as close to Gus as another human being was going to get. I'm sure there were times when she and I both felt left out." He rubbed his chin thoughtfully. "Charlie has been protective of my father, as only an older brother can be, for as long as I remember. He may be the elder by only a few minutes, but he doesn't take that responsibility lightly, believe me." He shrugged his shoulders. "Maybe they've stayed closer in their old age than a lot of twins since Charlie never married and my mother died. It's a shame, though, that Uncle Charlie has gotten a bit silly this past year or two."

"What about your father?"

Austin shook his head and chuckled. "Mentally, he's as sharp as a tack. And he likes a pretty girl, so watch out for him."

The Perry brothers didn't look anything like what she'd expected, Caroline had to admit as the two men finally strolled across the hotel lobby to join them. Perhaps it was because Austin was so tall and dark, in spite of his Nordic blue eyes, that she'd just assumed his father would be an older version of the same man.

Not so. Both Gus Perry and his twin brother couldn't be more than five feet nine inches tall. While Gus was still fairly trim, Charles Perry showed signs of typical male weight gain around the midriff. Both men were on the stocky side, with thinning gray hair and brown eyes. She could only conclude, Caroline decided as she and Austin stepped toward the approaching pair, that Austin took after his mother's side of the family.

Austin shook the first man's hand and then slipped an encouraging arm around Caroline's waist to bring her forward. "Dad, I'd like you to meet Mrs. Caroline Douglas. Honey, this is my father, Gus Perry."

She gave him a tentative smile and held out her hand. "Mr. Perry, how nice to meet you."

"Call me Gus," he grunted with a no-nonsense handshake.

"All right, Gus," she agreed a bit uneasily. She could feel his shrewd brown eyes taking in every detail of her, from her appearance to her manner of speaking. She didn't think he was missing a trick. Sharp as a tack, that's how Austin had described his father. He was undoubtedly right.

"And this is my Uncle Charlie," the younger man continued with genuine affection in his voice.

Caroline laughed lightly as the more portly brother pumped her hand enthusiastically and gave her a big smile. "Mr. Perry, it's a pleasure meeting you, too."

"The pleasure is all mine, Mrs. Douglas," he claimed as he beamed at her. "And the name is Charlie."

She looked from one brother to the other. "Then you must both call me Caroline, of course."

"Why don't we continue our conversation at lunch? I have a table reserved for eleven forty-five, and it's five minutes past that now," Austin pointed out as he herded them across the lobby toward the entrance to the restaurant.

The next fifteen or twenty minutes were spent settling in at a spacious corner table, selecting from the generous menu and placing their orders for drinks and lunch. The conversation continued over a beer for the men and a glass of white wine for Caroline. It touched on uncontroversial topics like the weather and the state of everyone's health and then moved on to a more animated discussion of Colorado's politics and history. It came as no surprise to Caroline that they eventually found themselves talking about the mining industry. After all, it was at the center of all three men's lives.

"Mining, it's all done by fancy equipment nowadays," Gus Perry said with a touch of disdain in his voice. "But I remember our grandfather telling Charlie and me, back when we were no more than knee-high to a grasshopper, how he started out with a pick and a shovel and an old wooden wheelbarrow."

His brother nodded his head and added to the story. "Grandpa said that in the beginning he worked with a candle spiked into a support timber in a shaft no better than a coyote hole."

"He had a mule named Jack," Gus went on, shaking his head. "That doggoned mule was with Shine for at least ten years. Maybe closer to fifteen."

"The other miners nicknamed Grandpa Shine," Charlie recalled, warming to the story. "As we were growing up, our grandpa must have told us a dozen different versions about how he got that nickname. He never did stick to the same story twice, though."

"By golly, he never did, did he?" Gus corroborated. "But I always had the feeling he got the nickname Shine once he found his first placer mine." Then he turned and looked straight at Caroline. "You ever been panning for gold, Mrs. Douglas?"

"Please, you promised to call me Caroline. And, no, I'm afraid I haven't."

"Nothing compares to the thrill of finding gold," Gus Perry told her, his dark eyes starting to shine. "I talked to a young fellow the other day who's part of an exploration company working a placer mine in a spring bed up in the mountains a couple of hours from here."

Austin interrupted long enough to explain to Caroline, "A placer mine is when you sift streambeds to find gold that's been washed down from the mountains. A so-called hard mine is when you go in and dig out gold-bearing rock."

"Anyway," Gus said, "this young fellow was telling me that they were using everything from fancy seismic instruments to old mining maps to helicopters to psychic dowsers to help them find where the gold was."

"Psychic dowsers?" Caroline repeated skeptically. She wasn't certain she'd heard him correctly.

"Remember old Timothy Lawton, that Indian dowser we hired back before the war?" Charlie interrupted, seeking confirmation from his younger brother.

"I sure do," Gus said, "but let me explain dowsing to the lady. You can see she doesn't understand what we're talking about." He turned back to his captive audience of one. "Some people had—some people still do have—this ability, this talent, for finding things. Things like gold and water and oil. And they use dowsing sticks to do it."

She quickly realized he was serious. "You mean like a tree branch, don't you?"

Austin's father nodded his balding head. "It could be a tree branch. I knew a dowser once who used a willow branch. He called his talent witching, and you had to wonder if it wasn't. I saw him walk around with that doggone willow branch in his hand, and when it dipped over a certain spot, he'd say, 'Dig here. Go down one hundred and fifty-seven feet.' And by golly, they went down one hundred and fifty-seven feet, and there was water rushing like an underground river." He shook his head as he remembered the incident. "But a dowsing stick can be made out of just about anything," he told her as he finished his meal. "Old Timothy had fashioned his out of plain metal coat hangers. He'd hold one stick in each hand and walk slowly along the bank of the stream where we had our placer mine. When the sticks crossed—" he slapped his hands together to illustrate "—that's where we knew to start dredging."

Charlie leaned back a little in his chair, lit up his cigar and decided to pick up the tale from there. "To get to one of our best placer mines, you had to drive up in the mountains, out a dusty dirt road, past a locked metal gate, then hike the last two or three miles over a rocky, narrow trail to a clear stream at the sixty-two-hundred-foot level."

"Really?" Caroline murmured, utterly fascinated.

From beside her, she heard what sounded like a faint groan of dismay. Then she caught the look Austin was giving her. It clearly said that by encouraging the brothers, she was asking to hear an endless stream of stories.

"Yup," Gus went on, as he, too, lit up a cigar. "But it was more like a four- or five-mile hike, wasn't it, Charlie? And I'm pretty sure the elevation of that particular mine was sixty-four-hundred feet."

"Maybe so. Maybe so," his twin muttered vaguely.

"Later on," Gus Perry said, speaking directly to Caroline again, "we hired a geologist to pore over old historical mining records. In fact, Austin used to work for us summers back when he was in college."

She turned to the handsome man beside her. "You never told me you studied geology in school."

"I don't think you ever asked. But I did, along with business administration. I was always more interested, however, in the commercial space-age metals like molybdenum."

Caroline's attention reverted to the older gentlemen. "Did it really work? I mean, Old Timothy and his dowsing sticks?"

"It sure did," Charlie piped up. "He found more than one rich deposit for Gus and me."

"Yup," his brother agreed. "Old Timothy Lawton was a legend in his own time, all right. He earned the fee we paid him in a real hurry. You might be interested in knowing that they still get a few old-timers dowsing even today."

She was and said so.

"Don't encourage them, or they'll start on the legends of the lost mines next," Austin said with something of a smile.

"My son, Jeremy, would love hearing your stories," she told the twin brothers. "He's always wanted to go panning for gold. Perhaps he'll have the chance to meet the two of you sometime."

"I'm sure he will," Austin interjected confidently.

Meanwhile his father was off on another tangent. "As you may know, Caroline, the price of gold rose sharply in the last decade. In some places up in the Sierra Nevada range of California, they claim as much as ninety-five percent of the mother lode is still there, virtually untouched." His eyes took on that sheen she was beginning to recognize. "Think of it, a fortune just waiting to be found."

"Gus and I have talked more than once about going out to California and trying our luck now that we're retired," Charlie confided to her. "To make a fortune in placer mining, all you've got to know is where the gold has washed down and settled in the last fifty thousand years or so. You just got to look and look and look some more."

"Even with modern technology, gold mining is still hard, physical labor," Austin reminded the two elderly men.

Gus Perry looked across the table at his only offspring. "Maybe so, son. But there's no thrill like picking up a big handful of dirt in your pan, dipping it into a flowing stream and then swirling it around until you can see the shiny gold flakes in the black silt. You used to understand that feeling when you were more of a miner and less of a businessman."

For a moment there was an uncomfortable silence around the table. Then Charlie Perry muttered, more to himself than to the others, "Gold. There isn't anything else quite like it, is there?"

Before anyone could respond, their waitress appeared and presented Austin with the check. "There's a telephone call for you, as well, Mr. Perry. It's your office. You can take the call by the front desk."

"Excuse me," Austin apologized to everyone at the table, but his words were especially meant for Caroline, and she knew it. "I'll only be gone a minute."

As soon as he disappeared around the corner of the lobby, Gus looked straight at Caroline. "I suppose Austin has told you that he's closing down some of the first mines our grandfather staked a claim to back before the turn of the century."

She suddenly felt as if she were on very shaky ground. "I believe he may have mentioned it."

"I don't understand why my own son would do such a thing," he complained bitterly. "Those mines are part of our family heritage. The Lucky Lady, the Silver Lady and all the others—they're what started the Perry Mining Company."

Caroline didn't want to be having this conversation with Gus Perry, but she wasn't about to listen to Austin being attacked without defending him, either. Even if the one doing the attacking was his own father.

"But I understand that the price of precious metals is far below its one-time high, and that makes it too costly to keep those particular mines in operation. After all, Perry Mining is no longer a privately held company, as it was in your day. As president of a public corporation, Austin is answerable to the stockholders who, in good faith, have invested their money in the Perry Mining Company. A public corporation and a private company have to be handled quite differently, you know," she pointed out as diplomatically as she could.

"Now what would a pretty young woman like you know about that kind of business?" Charlie spoke up.

It was Austin who answered for her. He had returned without any of them realizing it. "She knows quite a lot, actually, Uncle Charlie. Caroline is the president of her own company."

"It's small in comparison to Perry Mining, of course," she said modestly. "But I've learned a great deal about running a business. And speaking of business, I see it's time I was getting back to my office," she told them, glancing at her watch. She rose from her chair, and both older men followed suit. She held out her hand to Charles Perry first. "It was a pleasure joining you for lunch." She turned to Gus. "I'm very glad I had this opportunity to meet Austin's father. I think your son is a very special man. Now I know that it runs in the family."

Gus almost seemed to blush with pleasure. "I hope we'll meet again soon," he said, giving Caroline's hand a paternal pat.

It was after they had escorted both men safely to their cars that Austin finally stopped in the hotel parking garage and turned to her. "You stood up for me back there. Thank you."

"You're welcome," she replied just as politely.

"You were quite the charmer today, Mrs. Douglas," he went on in a slightly sardonic tone. "I'm not sure how you managed it, but you had both my father and my uncle eating out of your hand by the time lunch was half over."

She opened her handbag and took out her car keys. "They're both rather sweet men, actually."

"Sweet?" Austin roared. He put his head back and whooped with disbelieving laughter. "Obviously you haven't seen my father in action in the boardroom. He's about as sweet as a rattlesnake." He shook his head. "It's amazing what a couple of eccentric old coots like Gus and Charlie will do when there's a pretty woman around."

"I don't care what you say, I liked both of them. Oh, they might be a little rough around the edges, but I can sympathize with your father, Austin," she said earnestly. "He's one of those men determined to go down fighting because that's how he's survived all these years—by fighting for what was his." She looked up at him. "I understand why you have to do what you're doing, but in a way my heart goes out to Gus and Charlie, too."

"Then they are lucky, indeed," he said softly. Then he seemed determined to change the subject. "By the way, what are you doing this weekend? I thought we might find a drive-in movie theater somewhere and spend the evening necking in the back seat of my car."

She laughed self-consciously. "I can't this weekend, I'm afraid. I promised Jeremy that his best friend could sleep over."

"All weekend?" he said skeptically.

"No, just tomorrow night. But we have a little-league game and a picnic on Saturday, and we're driving up to Fort Collins to visit some cousins of my mother's on Sunday."

Austin stood up a little straighter. "Then what about sometime next week?"

She was already shaking her head. "I have a full schedule of business meetings next week, and I'm going out of town for several days to meet some new artists and suppliers."

"When will you be back?"

Caroline bristled. She wasn't used to answering to a man about her schedule. She wasn't sure she cared to start now. "I should be back on Saturday if everything goes as I've planned," she told him coolly.

"It doesn't seem like you have much time for us right now," Austin commented dryly.

Something in his tone made her look up at him. "I don't. I told you last weekend that this is my busiest season."

He didn't bother to disguise his displeasure at being put on hold. "Yes, you did, didn't you?"

She could tell he was upset with her. Frankly, the last thing she needed right now was for Austin to get all bent out of shape because she didn't have the time to go "parking" with him.

"I thought you understood how busy I was going to be." She knew she had made it sound like an accusation. But, damn it, he'd made a promise to her, and now he'd gone and deliberately broken that promise.

"Perhaps I understand better than you think," Austin retorted stonily.

Caroline took a sustaining breath. "You knew I had other responsibilities, other people to consider besides myself. I made that clear from our first date. And you agreed you were willing to give me some time."

"I thought I was. I'm not sure I realized what that might mean," he admitted with some reluctance.

Caroline went very still. "What are you trying to say?"

"I thought you needed time to know your own mind, your own heart about us, about you and me. I'm beginning to wonder if that's really the case."

"Go on," she gritted through her teeth, knowing she wasn't going to like what he intended to say next.

His voice hardened. "It seems to me, Caroline, that all you have time for is an occasional lover. You know, one who doesn't make too many demands on you or take up too much of your precious time."

She winced visibly. "That was an unkind thing to say."

"Yes, but it's the truth, isn't it?" He enunciated each word as if it were a dagger, a tiny dagger that plunged into her heart. "Maybe the real problem, Mrs. Douglas, is that you've been so busy being the perfect mother to your son, the always-thoughtful daughter to your parents, that you've forgotten how to be a real woman for a man."

Caroline paled beneath her makeup. She caught her lower lip between her teeth to keep it from trembling. "You're entitled to your opinion, of course. Now I really must be getting back to my office. I have a staff meeting at two o'clock. Thank you for lunch. I enjoyed meeting Charlie and Gus."

A muscle began to twitch in Austin's face. "Oh, hell," he muttered, driving his hand through his hair. "I don't want us to quarrel, Caroline."

"Neither do I," she confessed in a small voice.

"I'm trying," he grated.

"So am I," she said softly.

He sighed and squinted into the sun. "Sometimes you wonder how something that seems so right between two people can start to go so wrong."

"I know."

He bent over and dropped a cool kiss on her mouth. "I'll try to call you next weekend after you get back."

She swallowed. "All right."

She watched as Austin turned and walked toward his car. She couldn't help but wonder if he had any intention of trying to telephone her. She almost opened her mouth then and called to him, asking him to come back. But she hesitated, and he was gone without once looking back at her.

Despite Denver's unseasonably warm temperature for the first week of June, Caroline's hands were suddenly cold. As was her heart.

9

As THE AIRPLANE MADE its final approach to the runway, Caroline leaned back in her seat and stared out the small window beside her. She could feel the giant wheels touch down with a slight jerk and then the pressure of the brakes being applied. The big jet rattled and shook for a moment as it came to a stop before turning and taxiing up to the terminal.

Stapleton Airport was crowded, as it usually was on a Saturday in early June. School was out, and Caroline noted that the summer season in Colorado was in full swing. She dodged fresh-faced youths with knapsacks slung over their shoulders and young mothers with crying babies draped over theirs. She switched her briefcase and leather carryon to the other hand, grateful that she was spared the ordeal of having to wait in line at the crowded baggage carousels.

She was tired. Tired but happy. Well, perhaps *happy* wasn't the right word. Perhaps the right word was *pleased*. Yes, she was tired but pleased, Caroline decided as she switched hands again.

She had flown out early Thursday morning to see a list of clients and several exciting new artisans living and working in the Phoenix area. With temperatures soaring to the one-hundred-and-fifteen-degree mark, however, the Arizona heat had been oppressive. It had drained her energy, leaving her feeling like a wilted flower by the end of each day.

At least her efforts had proved fruitful, Caroline thought wearily, stopping to congratulate herself. She patted the samples she was bringing back in her briefcase. The miniature wood carvings should do especially well in this year's holiday shipments, if she was any judge. They were Native American primitives and quite different from anything Christmas by Caroline had offered before. As much as she hated being away from Jeremy, the trip had been worth it this time. That's what she told herself, anyway. Like most working mothers, she felt guilty when she put her business ahead of her child.

Without any trouble she located her blue station wagon in the airport parking lot. *Be grateful for small favors*, Caroline reminded herself as she tossed her briefcase and carryon in the back seat.

Every time she looked at her car now, she thought of Austin Perry. Not that that was the only time the man came to mind. In fact, it had shocked her to discover that she thought of him frequently, especially at night when she was alone in her bed.

The first time or two that had happened, she had tried to convince herself that it was only natural to wake up in the wee small hours of the night. This was her busiest season at the office, and she was under more stress than normal. Then she began to remember bits and pieces of her dreams, and she knew that her work had nothing to do with them. She dreamed of Austin.

Perhaps it wasn't so strange that she should find herself dreaming about him, Caroline acknowledged as she started for home. After all, Austin was the one who had reawakened her long-buried passions and physical desires. You couldn't shut off those kinds of wants and needs the way you could hot and cold running water.

Sometimes she wished she *could* just shut her emotions off, Caroline thought wistfully. Her life would be a whole lot easier. Since the afternoon of their lunch date with Gus and Charles Perry, she had agonized over every word Austin had said to her afterward. He'd been angry with her, she knew that, but it was still surprising how much his words had hurt. How deeply they had cut.

Of course, she couldn't help but think back, as well, to the night they had made love for the first time. That had been exactly two weeks ago. What was it Austin had said to her that Saturday evening at his home? "I've been thinking that we should consider a merger." And then not "Will you marry me?" but "I want to marry you."

Yes, that was exactly how he'd said it. Of course, he'd said a good many things that night. Things a man said when he wanted to get a woman into bed with him. She would be a fool to put too much stock in what was promised under those circumstances. And although he had admitted that he wanted to *make* love to her, he had never once said that he loved her. There was a world of difference between the two. Any woman knew that.

Lord, she was tired. Caroline sighed, keeping one hand on the steering wheel while she rubbed the back of her aching neck with the other. She was tired physically, mentally and emotionally. She was tired of not knowing her own mind, tired of not knowing her own heart.

On some level she wanted and needed Austin Perry, and that frightened her a little. But to want someone, to need someone in the physical sense of the word, wasn't enough. It never would be. After all, a woman's life wasn't spent in bed with a man.

The blare of an automobile horn interrupted her reverie. Caroline glanced in the rearview mirror at the car directly behind her and then up at the signal light. The man had no qualms about letting her know the stoplight had turned green. She'd better pay closer attention to her driving if she wanted to get home in one piece.

By the time she turned onto her own street, Caroline was more than ready for a hot soak in the bathtub. A long, leisurely bath, a glass of wine and a good night's sleep. That's what she really needed to feel human again!

As she pulled into the driveway beside her house, she noticed there was a Jeep parked across the street. It looked familiar. She only knew one person who drove a four-door Jeep and that, of course, was Austin Perry.

"Oh, damn!" she swore softly. Austin was the last person she wanted to confront right now. Why couldn't he have waited and called her as he had said he would?

She unlocked the front door to her house and set her briefcase and carryon down in the hallway before calling out, "Is anybody home?"

There was no answer. She stuck her head around the corner of the living room and found it empty. Then she heard voices coming from the back of the house, somewhere in the vicinity of the family room or the kitchen.

Unsuspectingly, Caroline opened the kitchen door. Her jaw dropped, and she simply stood still for a minute or two. She couldn't believe her eyes. As a matter of fact, she nearly turned and went out again, thinking she'd walked into the wrong house! She must be in the wrong house, she tried to tell herself calmly. But she knew she wasn't.

"What in the world?" she finally managed, shaking her head.

Her usually immaculate kitchen was an unholy mess! It looked as if a tornado had ripped through sometime in the past ten minutes. There were dirty pots and pans and sticks of melting butter and spilled sugar and clumps of dough everywhere. And topping the whole mess off was a fine layer of white flour. Caroline didn't know whether to laugh or cry. In the end, she did neither.

"Mother! Dad! Jeremy!" she bellowed as she stepped around a puddle of unknown origin on the tile floor and stalked into the family room.

The room was empty, but the sliding glass doors leading to the patio were standing wide open.

She marched toward them. "Jeremy?"

"Hi, Mom! We're out here!" he called to her from the backyard.

"Hello, Caroline," came the more formal greeting from the man sitting in the lawn chair next to her son.

They were both dressed in old T-shirts, faded blue jeans and sneakers that had seen better days. And they each held a baseball mitt in one hand.

For a moment Caroline was speechless. Even knowing Austin was going to be here hadn't prepared her for seeing him again. "Austin? What are you doing here?" She turned her attention to Jeremy before the man had a chance to answer her. "And what, may I ask, has happened to my kitchen?"

That seemed to get their undivided attention. Both pairs of blue eyes were on her now.

"Well, Austin and I got hungry for something good to eat," Jeremy began, then swallowed hard. "We were going to clean up the mess before you got home, Mom, honest we were, but we got busy playing baseball and . . ."

"Maybe I better explain it to your mother, Jeremy," Austin suggested as he unfolded his long legs and rose from the lawn chair.

"Yes, maybe you better," Caroline gritted through her teeth as he joined her inside the house. "In there." She pointed to the kitchen. "Well perhaps not in there," she amended in a murderous tone, looking at the mess. "Let's try the front hall, shall we?" She did an about-face and swept past him through the doorway.

Austin followed and closed the door discreetly behind them. "Now, Caroline, don't go getting your dander up."

"Don't you 'now, Caroline' me, Austin Perry!" she exploded. "And I'll get my dander up if I want to."

He raked his fingers through his dark hair. "I'm sorry about the disaster in your kitchen, but we intended to clean it up, as Jeremy said. We just hadn't gotten around to it yet."

She stood there and glared at him. "I would like an explanation of what is going on here, and I would like it now."

His eyes narrowed for an instant. "Like Jeremy told you, we got hungry. We couldn't find anything in the house to snack on, so we decided to make ourselves some cookies."

"That's not what I meant. I would like an explanation of your presence in my home and with my son."

Austin's face darkened momentarily. "I didn't think my presence here required an explanation."

"I think it does," she declared haughtily. "I don't care for people who sneak into my house behind my back."

"I wasn't sneaking anywhere behind your back," he informed her evenly. "For your information, Jeremy invited me over with Edna and Harry's permission."

An expression of disbelief flickered across her face. "My son called you up and invited you to come over?"

"No. Not exactly," he said as if he weren't used to having his motives, let alone his actions, questioned. "Actually, I called to talk to you. Jeremy answered the telephone, and he told me you weren't home from the airport yet. We got talking. I asked him what he was doing today. He said nothing because all of his friends were busy or gone away on vacation. He wanted to know if I could come over and play a little baseball with him. I said sure, but he better check with his grandparents first." Caroline began to tap her foot impatiently.

"Anyway, apparently Edna and Harry thought it was a good idea. When I got here, they decided to go play a round of golf with some friends who'd invited them out earlier." He took a deep breath before he continued. "We played catch for a while in the back yard, and then Jeremy and I decided we were hungry. We couldn't find anything in the house to nibble on, so we decided to bake ourselves some cookies. Snickerdoodles, to be exact." At that, Austin smiled, but he wasn't smiling at her. She realized that. "It was fun, too. And the cookies weren't bad, either. Unfortunately, we can't offer you any. I'm afraid between the two of us, Jeremy and I ate them all."

Caroline's shoulders drooped imperceptibly. "I don't care about the cookies. I don't even care about the awful mess you made in my kitchen. What I do care about is your coming into my home and trying to ingratiate yourself with my family."

"Ingratiate myself?" he repeated harshly.

"Yes, ingratiate yourself."

He stared at her. "And how do you propose that I'm doing that?" he asked incredulously.

"By assuming the role of a thoughtful son-in-law and indulgent father, by telling my parents it was all right to run off and play golf, by throwing a baseball around in the back yard with Jeremy, by baking his favorite cookies with him—"

Austin threw his hands up in the air. "I don't believe this! I don't believe you're accusing me of—of trying to seduce your own family!" Then his eyes narrowed, and his gaze grew shrewd. "Do you know what I think, Mrs. Douglas?" he said, pointing a finger at her. "I think it's plain old-fashioned jealousy. I think you're pea-green with it because of the relationship I have with your mother and father, and especially with Jeremy."

Red cheeked, she swung away from him, turning to face in the opposite direction. "That is the most ridiculous thing I have ever heard!" she protested vehemently.

"No, it isn't. Be honest with yourself, Caroline. Didn't you feel even the slightest twinge of jealousy just now when you saw your son and me together?"

"No!" she shot back.

"Yes!" he insisted, reaching out to take hold of her. His hands closed around her shoulders as he turned her to face him. "I know how you feel, Caroline. I know because I've felt that way, too," he explained gently. "I was envious of how easily you seemed to get along with my father and uncle the day we all had lunch together. I couldn't help but think of all the times I'd tried—and failed—to have that kind of relaxed conversation with them." She straightened her shoulders, and he dropped his hands. "It can work both ways, you know. So don't accuse me of trying to sneak into your house and role-play behind your sweet back when that's not what's really bothering you."

Fatigue and strain had shorn Caroline of her usual defenses. "But that is what's bothering me," she breathed through her teeth. "You know how important my son's happiness is to me, Austin. And I believe that you're fully capable of using Jeremy to get to me, whether you realize it or not. He already looks up to you and admires you. You know he adores you. It won't take much more, and he'll start thinking of you as a father substitute."

"And would that be so very bad?" he asked carefully.

"It could be disastrous for Jeremy if things don't work out between us," she told him bluntly. "I've tried to make my position clear about our relationship, but you keep pressuring me into more than I'm ready for. I know my parents are on your side, but I feel like you're using them and my son to manipulate me. In my book, that's playing dirty pool, Austin."

He stood there looking thoughtfully out the front window for a minute or two. "You have a serious problem, Caroline, in my book, if you think I'm only interested in Jeremy or in Edna and Harry as a means of convincing you to marry me."

"Try *forcing* me to marry you. That's closer to the truth."

Austin turned surprisingly sad eyes on her. She hadn't ever expected to see such sadness in those blue eyes of his.

"Did it ever occur to you, Caroline, that I'm envious of the family you seem to take for granted? You've got something that I've never had and probably never will have: a good, solid, happy family life. There's so much love between all of you, even when you're angry with each other." He rubbed a weary hand across his eyes. "I swear to you that I never intentionally used Jeremy or your parents as a means of trying to get to you. I had no idea my presence here today would upset you so much."

"I know you didn't." She finally relented, her heart suddenly aching for both of them.

Austin spread his hands in a futile gesture. "And I have to admit that I don't understand why you won't marry me. Most women get upset when a man doesn't want to marry them. You seem to be mad at me because I do." He shook his head. "Damned if I can figure it out."

Caroline took a deep breath and decided to try to explain. "Have you ever heard of an avadavat?"

He shook his head. "No."

"Well, it's a small bird of India, kept as a caged pet for its singing ability. I can't bear to see things put in cages, Austin, and that includes anything from a small bird to a human being." Her voice throbbed with the force and sincerity of her emotions. He seemed taken aback. "What most men really want when they decide to marry and take a wife is a kind of caged avadavat to sing for them. The man controls what kind of cage she lives in and when she's fed and even if she's allowed out of her cage. In short, he runs her life." Caroline struggled to keep her voice even. "That Saturday night at your home something very special happened between us. But when it came right down to the final word, you didn't *ask* how I felt about marriage. You *told* me that you wanted to marry me." He took a step toward her, and she held out a hand to ward him off. "I will marry again only if and when *I'm* ready to get married, Austin Perry. I will not be bulldozed into it by anyone, and that includes you."

He made an imposing figure standing there in the hallway of her home, the late-afternoon sun at his back. "All right," he said quietly, "I'm not bulldozing this time. I'm asking. Will you marry me?"

Her eyes were dark with regret as she murmured, "No, I won't. I can't."

The expression on his face was both bewildered and watchful. "Why can't you?"

Caroline took a deep breath. "Because there's something very important missing between us, Austin." She could see he didn't have the slightest idea what she was talking about. She went on. "We've talked about wanting each other and needing each other and even about marrying each other. But we have never once said anything about loving each other."

He frowned and looked at her. "Love? Is that what this is all about?"

Her heart was pounding. "Of course."

He took a step toward her. "But I told you a couple of weeks ago that I've wanted to make love with you since that first night in my cabin."

Caroline stuck to her guns. "You're talking about sex. I'm talking about love."

"But I know you love me," he claimed confidently. "You must love me. A woman like you isn't capable of one without the other."

"And why not?" she challenged. "A man is fully capable of separating the physical act from the emotional commitment. Why should a woman be any different when it comes to sexual wants and needs?"

Austin raked a frustrated hand through his already rumpled hair and swore under his breath. "You've got me going in so many directions at once that I don't know where I am anymore! I don't know what you want from me. I don't think *you* know what you want, either." He pointed an accusing finger at her. "You're right about one thing, Mrs. Douglas. You are a coward. You've used everything in the book as a excuse, as a smoke screen to cover up the real reason you won't marry me. You're afraid. You're afraid to take a chance. When I came along, you were ready for a love affair, Caroline, but you weren't ready for love."

Her eyes grew wide and dark with anger. "Why, you overbearing, sanctimonious, male chauvinist know-it-all—"

"Mom? Austin?"

They both turned and saw Jeremy standing in the doorway between the kitchen and the hallway. There was a stricken expression on his young face, and his eyes were huge and wide. Then he pushed past them and took the stairs two at a time as fast as his long, thin legs would carry him.

Caroline looked back at Austin. "There, are you satisfied? Look what you've done!"

He grabbed her by the arm as she started to go after Jeremy. "No! Look what *you've* done!"

She broke loose and was halfway up the flight of stairs when she heard him call out to her.

"And the only cage around you, Caroline Douglas, is the one you put there yourself!"

She looked down at him. "Go away, Austin. Just go away." Then she ran up the last few steps.

She found the door of Jeremy's room shut. There was a poster taped to it that said No Adults Allowed Unless Accompanied by a Child. Caroline took a deep breath and knocked on the door of her son's bedroom. "Jeremy, it's Mom."

A minute later a small voice called out, "Come in, Mom."

She opened the door and saw him stretched out on his bed, his back to her. He seemed to be staring out the window. She frantically searched her mind for the words she should say.

Poor Jeremy. He had no precedent for what he had just seen and heard between two consenting adults. He had never known a mother and father to have a disagreement. Caroline suddenly realized that her son had led a sheltered life in some ways. The world wasn't always champagne and roses between a man and a woman, and he was just finding that out for the first time. She supposed he had heard his friends talk about their parents and fights and divorce, but it wasn't the same thing as seeing and hearing it firsthand.

Caroline sat down on the edge of his bed and rested a hand lightly on his arm. "I know that we—that I have upset you."

He turned over and looked up at her. "What were you and Austin fighting about? Why were you shouting at each other?"

"Oh, Jeremy," she sighed and stared down at her hands. "Even people who love each other sometimes fight and sometimes shout at one another. I love you and you love me, but we get mad at each other sometimes, don't we?"

Now, at least, they were back on familiar ground. "Yeah, I guess so," he admitted grudgingly. He sat up on the bed and wrapped his arms around his knees. "Does that mean you and Austin love each other?"

Here it was, Caroline realized, staring her straight in the face at last. Jeremy wasn't a little boy anymore. He was a thinking, feeling human being, and he deserved the truth from her. But did she know what the truth was?

She looked into his eyes. "Yes, I think Austin and I love each other, but we have some problems, problems we're not sure we can work out."

Jeremy looked at her with a wisdom that children sometimes possessed because of their uncluttered view of the world and its people. "If you love Austin and he loves you, then the two of you should get married."

"If it were only that simple," she murmured, smoothing out the wrinkles in the bedspread. "Whatever happens, I want you to know that I love you, Jeremy, and I always will. You are my son. My one and only. But you'll grow up and go away to college someday. Then you'll get a job and live in an apartment. One day you'll find the right woman and get married and have a family of your own. And I'll be all alone," she whispered.

Jeremy threw his arms around her neck and squeezed her hard. "I'll stay with you, Mom!"

The tears sparkled like silver dew on her dark lashes. "Oh, darling, you can't. Everybody has to grow up and move away from home sometime. You will, too. You should. You'll want to by the time you're eighteen. And I'll want you to go, too. It's all a natural part of growing up."

The boy sat back on his heels. "Why are you crying, Mom? You said you liked your life. You said you were happy."

"I am happy in many ways, but I suddenly realized that this may be my last chance for a different kind of happiness, Jeremy." Caroline quickly dried her tears and patted his arm. "But that's enough sad talk. What did you and Austin do this afternoon? Besides play baseball and make one awful mess of the kitchen?"

He looked a little sheepish and then said, "I hope you and Austin stay friends, Mom. He promised to take me to see a Broncos game next fall. He's got season's tickets. And we're going panning for gold tomorrow morning, way up in the mountains. Just the two of us. That is, if it's all right with you."

Caroline knew she didn't have the heart to say no. "Of course it's all right with me."

Jeremy sat up straighter then, his eyes bright with excitement. "Austin says it's best to go panning for gold in the late spring or early summer once the snow starts melting off the mountains because it carries a lot of rocks and minerals downstream."

"I'm sure he would know about that kind of thing. He's the president of a mining company, you know. He has a log cabin up in the mountains that you'd like, too."

Jeremy nodded his head. "Yeah, Austin told me about that. When he was a kid, he used to go panning for gold all the time up near that cabin. But he went by himself. His father didn't have time to do much with him, I guess. Anyway, he had this little container he kept his gold dust in. He said it took him five years to get it filled to half an inch. He says you hardly ever find gold nuggets. Can you imagine all that work for half an inch of gold dust, Mom?"

"No, I can't," she said a little sadly.

"Of course, Austin says it's more than just the gold. He says he likes to tramp around in the woods and hike up the mountains and get out in the fresh air." Then Jeremy added in a wistful voice, "And be by himself or maybe with a good friend."

Caroline felt her heart contract and her eyes grow full. "What else did you and Austin talk about this afternoon?"

The boy looked thoughtful for a moment. "We talked about the Broncos, of course, and what sports we liked. We both like baseball the best and football second best. Austin talked about his father, too. I don't think he got along very well with his dad when he was a kid. But he told me he'd always wanted a son, but that he didn't know much about being a father." Two big blue eyes looked at Caroline. "I told Austin that was okay because I didn't know much about having a father."

For a moment Caroline couldn't seem to breathe. What could anyone have said that could have touched her more than that?

How could Austin know anything about loving a woman the way she needed to be loved? What would he know about being a husband? For crying out loud, the man was a thirty-eight-year-old bachelor. She'd been married once a long time ago, and yet she didn't know much about being a wife, either. But surely, surely, they could learn together!

"I'm sorry you heard Austin and me quarreling, Jeremy. We didn't mean to upset you. Are you all right now?"

"Sure I am, Mom."

She grinned at him. "Good! Then you can come help me clean up that awful mess you two guys made in the kitchen before your grandparents get back from their golf game. Can you imagine the expression on your grandmother's face if she saw the kitchen the way it looks right now?"

Jeremy laughed loudly. "Grandma would faint."

"To say the very least." His mother chuckled under her breath as the two of them headed downstairs.

IT WAS A GOOD TWO HOURS later before Caroline found herself soaking in a tubful of hot water and her favorite bubble bath. Her hair was pinned on top of her head, and there was a glass of white wine within easy reach.

She pressed a warm washcloth to her face and breathed in deeply. She was so tired, and it felt so good just to lie here. She let the heat and moisture soak the tension and the weariness from her bones and muscles. But out of nowhere the tears began. They flowed down her face silently in streams.

Tears were such funny things. There were tears of joy and awe, like the tears she had shed at Jeremy's birth. There were tears of pride and honor. Those tears came whenever the national anthem was played. There were tears of anger, tears of humiliation, tears of sorrow. She had known them all. There were tears of immeasurable sadness and tears that came when love was gone.

"The days were all alike when love has gone." Caroline couldn't seem to remember who had said that, but in some ways she supposed it was true. It was a truth she would have to face. She would be alone one day, perhaps, and then each day would become like the next. It didn't mean she had to be alone now. That was her decision and hers alone.

She had let Austin go. In fact, she had *told* him to go. She had rejected him out of pride and out of an almost compulsive need to stay in control of her own life. Perhaps the way to take real control of her life was to make up her own mind about the man. After all, her feelings were the only thing that mattered, in the end.

Taking another sip of her wine, Caroline slipped down into the steaming water until only her head and neck were visible.

What did she feel for Austin Perry?

She closed her eyes, and he was suddenly there. Did she love him? She certainly loved the way he looked and the way he smelled. She loved the rich sound of his laughter and the deep baritone of his voice. She loved the way he kissed her, the way he touched her, the way he thrilled her. She loved the taste of him and the touch of his skin, his hair, his masculine strength.

She loved his wit and his intelligence. She loved the blue color of his eyes, which was so much like Jeremy's. She loved the shape of his ears and the way the soft, dark hair curled at the back of his neck. And she loved the way he made love to her.

She loved him. She took another sip of wine and decided to say it out loud. "I love you, Austin Perry."

And somehow, in saying it aloud, Caroline finally knew it was true. She did love Austin.

She imagined herself as she would be in ten years, in twenty years, without the love of a good man. She didn't like what she saw.

"Well, Caroline Davis Douglas, are you a woman or a mouse? If you're so determined to be in control of your life, if you love the man as much as you say you do, then what are you going to do about it?"

She was still asking herself that question as she dried off and slipped into a nightgown and robe. When she went to join her family downstairs a few minutes later, she found her mother reading the latest issue of *Ladies' Home Journal*. Her father was absorbed in some early-evening game show on television. Jeremy was outside playing touch football with a group of neighborhood children. Caroline stood in the doorway for a moment and then loudly cleared her throat. Two pairs of eyes looked up at her.

She took the plunge. "I want the two of you to know that I love Austin Perry and that I'm going to marry him if he still feels the same way about us after the awful row we had this afternoon. And I plan to tell him exactly how I feel just as soon as he and Jeremy get back from their outing tomorrow."

There was a moment of polite—or perhaps it was stunned—silence from the pair sitting on the sofa.

"I hope everything works out between the two of you," Edna remarked. "You and Austin make a lovely couple." Then she went back to reading her magazine.

"That's great news, dear," Harry chipped in before his attention reverted to the contestants and the big wheel they kept spinning.

Caroline looked past them to the sliding glass doors at the rear of the house. "Well, isn't anyone going to tell me that I'm crazy or something?"

"You're old enough to know your own mind," her father said. "By the way, we've been invited to spend a few days at our friends', the Wilsons', home in Colorado Springs."

Edna glanced up from her magazine. "You remember the Wilsons, don't you, dear?"

"Yes, of course I do. When are you planning to leave?"

"We thought we'd drive up tomorrow and return sometime later in the week," Harry explained.

"That will give you all day tomorrow to yourself," Edna pointed out. "We both think you could use a day without anyone else around. You've been working so hard. After your trip, you must be exhausted."

Caroline yawned. "I am tired. It was so hot in Phoenix, and I didn't sleep very well. As a matter of fact, would you mind terribly if I went to bed now?"

"You go straight to bed this minute," her mother ordered out of genuine concern. "We'll see that Jeremy gets tucked in. As a matter of fact, we'll see him off in the morning so you can sleep in. He and Austin were talking on the telephone earlier this evening, and it sounds like they're planning to make an early start of it."

"Good night, then," Caroline managed in a voice barely above a whisper as she swayed wearily on her feet.

"Good night, Caroline," her father called out.

"Pleasant dreams, dear," her mother threw in as an afterthought.

After their daughter had left the room, Edna looked over at her husband. "Oh, Harry, what'll we do? She looks so tired and so alone."

Harry Davis patted his wife's hand consolingly. "Austin Perry's a good man, Edna. She won't be alone for long."

"Do you really believe that?"

"Yes, I do. But it wouldn't hurt if we said a special prayer for her, too."

"Yes, we'll do that."

"In the end, that's all any parent can do," Harry conceded as he gazed after his beloved daughter.

10

"DO YOU REALLY THINK we'll find any gold, Austin?" Jeremy asked eagerly as the Jeep continued to climb along the steep mountain road.

"We might find a little gold dust if we're lucky. But like I told you on the drive up here, chances are we won't find any real nuggets," Austin gently reminded the boy sitting beside him. He looked up at the clear Colorado sky, squinting into the bright sunlight. "At least we lucked out and got good weather today."

"Yeah, it's pretty neat up here," the boy admitted as they drove by clumps of silver-barked aspen and majestic, tree-studded mountains and blue morning air still clinging to the green meadow grasses.

Austin smiled at Jeremy. "Yes, it is pretty neat. I've got a log cabin not more than a mile or two from here, you know."

Jeremy nodded his curly head. "Mom said you did." He went on to ask, "Is all of this land yours?"

"Some of it. But most of it's government land reserved as national forests."

"Do you think we'll see any wild animals, like a bobcat or a cougar—" Jeremy's eyes were growing wider and wider "—or maybe a herd of wild mustangs?"

The corners of Austin's mouth lifted in amusement. "I don't think we'll see any of those, but we might catch sight of a river otter or a grouse or perhaps a small herd of mule deer."

"T-ou-gh!" the boy exclaimed, enlarging his favorite word to three syllables.

Their conversation reverted to more practical matters. "Did you remember to bring a pair of mittens or warm gloves like I told you?" Austin glanced down at the knapsack on the seat beside Jeremy.

"Yessir. And I brought an extra jacket and my rubber boots just like you said."

"Good," he said, nodding his approval. "It can get chilly at this altitude, even in the summertime. Believe me, your hands, especially the tips of your fingers, will feel like they're half frozen after they've been in icy stream water coming down off one of those snow-capped mountains."

"I won't mind," Jeremy declared bravely.

He had once been a lot like this boy, Austin thought. He hadn't cared at that age, either. Kids could display an incredible amount of resilience when they wanted or needed something badly enough.

"We'll park the Jeep over there," he said, indicating a level area off to one side of the track. "Then we'll hike the rest of the way. It's only a short distance from here to my favorite spot along the stream."

Jeremy opened the passenger's door and jumped down. "Will I need my knapsack now?"

"Better bring it with you. I've got some more equipment in the back, too," Austin said, walking around to the rear of the vehicle. He took out a standard pick, a small shovel, a waterproof tarpaulin and two shallow, handleless pans. Then he rummaged in the pocket of his insulated vest and brought out a small vial. He handed it to Jeremy. "This is yours to keep. Just in case you get lucky your first time out and find some gold."

From the expression on Jeremy's face, you would have thought Austin had just given him a long-hoped-for present.

"Gee, thanks, Austin," he said with feeling.

"You're welcome, Jeremy. Now are you ready to get started?"

"Yessir!"

"Then you grab the gold pans and that thermos of hot coffee. I'll bring the pick, the shovel and the tarp. I think we'll leave our lunch in the Jeep for now." He glanced down at the boy's slender body. "You had breakfast before you left home this morning, didn't you?"

Jeremy raised his blue eyes heavenward. "Grandma made me eat all kinds of junk before she'd let me come."

"Junk?" Austin queried.

He made a face. "Yeah, you know, eggs and bacon and toast and a gigantic glass of milk."

Austin's tanned face suddenly dissolved into a smile. "If I'd known your grandmother was going to make all that 'junk,' I would have come over for breakfast myself."

But the last thing Jeremy was interested in discussing was food. He had more important matters on his mind. "What if I did find some gold, Austin, would it be worth real money? I mean, what if it was no more than that much?" he asked, pinching his thumb and forefinger together.

"I say, you'd have to save up quite a few pinches before it would be worth it to exchange your gold for cash."

"I guess you're right." Jeremy looked off toward the mountains, and his expression became dreamlike. "I wonder how much gold was worth in the old days."

Austin slung his pack over his shoulder, picked up the shovel, the pick and the tarpaulin and started off in the direction of the stream. "I guess that depends on what you mean by the old days. Way back in the 1850s, they used to say that a pinch of gold dust was worth about one dollar."

Jeremy looked down at his fingers again and then started after the man. "A pinch was worth a dollar?"

"Yup. Then for a long time the government kept the price of gold fixed at thirty-five dollars an ounce. When that was changed about six or seven years ago, the price soared to nearly nine hundred dollars an ounce. Now it usually fluctuates between three and four hundred dollars, sometimes a little higher."

"Wow! You know everything about stuff like that, don't you?"

"No matter how much you think you know about something, Jeremy, there's always somebody who knows more. When it comes to mining, I know more than most people but less than others. After all, mining is my business."

"Mom says you studied geology in college, and now you're president of a mining company," Jeremy said as they tramped along.

"Your mom's right."

"Maybe I'll study geology when I'm old enough to go away to college."

Austin smiled down at him. "Maybe you will, but you've got a while before you have to decide." He stopped and lowered his load to the ground. "We'll spread the tarp out here. That way we can set our equipment on it or even sit down on it ourselves in case the ground's damp."

When they had finished setting up camp, Austin straightened to his full height of more than six feet and stretched his long arms above his head. He inhaled deeply and let his eyes close for a moment, savoring the peace and tranquility of this place. When he opened them again, he caught a glimpse of the boy beside him, arms stretched above his thin-set shoulders and curly head of hair, eyes closed. Austin smiled to himself and looked away until he heard Jeremy whistling under his breath as he dug around in his knapsack.

"Hey, Austin, I brought my compass in case we decide to go exploring," he announced as he slipped it into the pocket of his blue jeans. "Is there an old cave or a ghost town or anything really neat to explore around here?"

"There's an abandoned mine shaft over on the other side of that ridge. I used to explore parts of it when I was younger." When he was a lot younger, Austin admitted to himself.

Jeremy looked up at him. "Have you ever seen a *real* ghost town?"

"Sure. Haven't you?"

"Nope, but I'll bet it was neat."

Austin reached out and rested his hand on the boy's shoulder for a moment. "Maybe I can show you one sometime. We've got plenty of them in this part of Colorado, if you know where to look. They're usually hidden back up in the hills. Don't be disappointed, though. A ghost town is usually no more than a few weathered buildings and a wagon or two with the wood rotting through, maybe some rusty nails and horseshoes lying around, or bits of colored glass and an old, long-forgotten cemetery."

"How come nobody lives there anymore?"

"They were boomtowns, Jeremy. People came there for the gold or silver or copper. When the gold and silver and copper were gone, the people left, too." Austin gazed into the distance as if looking at something on the horizon. "There are always stories going around about the lost mines. I remember hearing one from my father when I was about your age. It was about a lost ledge of silver. Supposedly, over a hundred years ago three or four men claimed to have seen it. They even brought back samples of the ore. But when they tried to go back and locate the ledge of silver, they never could find it again."

The boy was all eyes and ears. "Why not?"

"There were too many mountains and hills and dry washes that all looked alike, I guess. They hunted for years and years, but they never could find the same place again. That's the kind of thing that can drive a man crazy. I think a few of the old-timers probably did go a little mad."

"You mean they were sick?"

"In a way. It was all they thought about or talked about—finding that lost ledge of silver or some legendary gold mine they were convinced was always just around the next mountain. It was like a fever that got in their blood."

"I guess that wasn't too healthy," Jeremy concluded.

"I'm sure it wasn't. Too much of anything isn't healthy, even if it's too many snickerdoodle cookies," Austin teased him, trying to lighten the tone of their conversation. "What do you say, partner? Are you ready to try your hand at panning for gold?"

"I sure am!"

"The first thing we better do is put on our rubber boots," Austin instructed as he opened his pack and took his out. Once they had their feet protected from the wet, he handed Jeremy one of the pans. "Now, when you're looking by a stream like we're going to, the best places to find gold are in crevices—that's a small crack or opening along the bank. Another good place is near grass or tree roots."

"In case some gold got stuck in a root or something while it was washing downstream."

Austin gave him an approving nod. "Exactly. Now pick a spot by the edge of the stream, scoop up some sand and water and swirl it in your pan like I'm doing." He demonstrated what seemed to be a simple technique. "Keep doing that over and over until you're sure you don't see anything kind of bright and shiny in your pan. Remember, it may be no more than a fleck. Once you're sure there's nothing in your pan, dump it to one side and try again."

With the tip of his tongue caught between his teeth, concentrating for all he was worth, Jeremy gave it a try. "Am I doing it right, Austin?" he asked a few attempts later.

"You sure are, partner. Although I've heard it said that no two people pan exactly alike."

The boy glanced up for an instant. "You mean kind of like no two people have exactly the same fingerprints."

"Yes, just like that," he agreed as they went back to work.

It was some time later that morning, as they squatted near the tarpaulin sharing a cup of hot coffee, that Jeremy looked over at the man beside him and said in a quiet voice, "Do you mind if I ask you a question?"

Austin gazed into the blue eyes that were hauntingly like his own. "No, I don't mind if you ask me a question, Jeremy."

The boy opened his mouth and blurted it out quickly as though half afraid he might lose his nerve. "Do you think it will work out between you and my mom?"

Austin took a deep breath. "I hope so. I really hope so, Jeremy."

"So do I," the boy echoed with a tentative smile. Then he was on to another subject. "Do you think we could take a few minutes and just look in that old mine shaft? I've never seen what the inside of one looks like."

"I don't see why not," Austin replied, finishing off his coffee and putting the lid back on the thermos. "I'll have to check it out first, of course. I haven't been inside that particular mine for a couple of years. We'll have to see if the support timbers are still solid."

"I'll bring my compass," Jeremy volunteered, jumping to his feet.

"It wouldn't hurt to bring your jacket, as well. It might be cold down in the shaft. We'll need a couple of hard hats and a high-powered flashlight from the back of the Jeep, too."

"We don't have to wear our rubber boots, do we?" Jeremy complained as he trod behind Austin, trying to keep up with his long-legged stride.

"No. We can leave them in the Jeep until we get back."

"Now," Austin was explaining to him a few minutes later as they stood by the entrance to the mine, "I'm going ahead a few feet and test some of the supports. I want you to stay put until I come back for you. Do you understand?"

"Yessir, I understand. I'll stay right here."

"Good. I won't be gone long," Austin assured him before he disappeared into the shadowy passageway. He reappeared less than ten minutes later as promised and gave Jeremy the thumbs-up sign. "Everything looks good and solid in there. Remember to keep your hard hat on at all times and stay close to me. We'll follow the old ore car tracks, but we won't go into the shaft more than forty or fifty feet. That should be enough to give you a good idea of what the inside of a mine is like. Do you have any questions before we start?"

Jeremy shook his head. "No."

Austin went first, with Jeremy right behind him. The beam from the flashlight created a kind of eerie impression as it bounced off the wooden support timbers and the craggy rock formations surrounding the track on all three sides. There was dirt and sand and a few odd pieces of timber and rock underfoot.

When they'd gone about forty feet inside the tunnel, Austin came to a halt and turned. "I think this is far enough," he said in a quiet but authoritative voice.

They stood side by side and looked back at the bright sunlight illuminating the entrance to the mine.

"It doesn't look so—scary from here, does it?" Jeremy said in a small voice.

"It's not scary, Jeremy, if you're careful and if you know what you're doing. It's the unknown that frightens most people."

"I'm not scared as long as I'm with you," the boy confessed, moving a step closer to the big man.

Then it happened. And it was the oddest thing. At that moment the short, fine hairs on the back of Austin's neck stood straight on end. He could never remember having a feeling quite like that before. It wasn't exactly a premonition; it was more like some vague sixth sense warning him that something wasn't quite right about this place. He didn't want to panic the boy, but he took him firmly by the arm and said, "I think we should get out of here now, Jeremy."

They started back toward the entrance to the mine; they had gone some ten or fifteen feet when it happened. In no more than a split second, they heard a tremendous explosion—and then the entrance to the mine collapsed before their very eyes.

CAROLINE SLUMPED DOWN in the chair by the telephone and said in an unnaturally calm voice, "Mr. Perry, would you mind repeating what you just told me?"

"The authorities have just notified me, Caroline. There has been some kind of accident up at the old mine near Austin's property. The entrance apparently collapsed, and they believe Austin and Jeremy are trapped inside the mine shaft."

Caroline was still holding her breath. She exhaled and whispered out of sheer desperation, "Are they sure?"

"As sure as they can be. Austin's Jeep is parked nearby. There's a boy's knapsack and mittens on the front seat and two pairs of rubber boots in the back."

She bit down hard on her lip. It was some twenty or thirty seconds before she could ask, "How did the authorities find out there had been an accident?"

The man's voice quavered. "That's the strange part, I'm afraid. They received an anonymous tip over the telephone telling them exactly *what* had happened and *where*."

Suddenly Caroline began to shake. "In other words, it may not have been an accident."

"That's the way it's beginning to look," Gus Perry stated grimly.

"Oh, Gus, do you think this has anything to do with those letters Austin was getting a few weeks ago?" An icy-cold chill was fingering its way up her spine, vertebra by vertebra.

For a minute there was only stunned silence on the other end of the telephone. Then, "What letters?"

She groaned. "Austin never told you?"

"No, he never told me," his father said in a voice that had aged years in a matter of seconds.

Caroline swallowed the sickening taste in her mouth. "There were only two letters that I know of. Both were vaguely worded. But they warned Austin not to close down the mines, specifically the Lucky Lady and the Silver Lady. He did mention a rash of annoying telephone calls, but those stopped some time ago, too."

"I wish I'd known about all this. Why didn't Austin tell me?"

"Perhaps he didn't want to worry you," Caroline suggested, circumventing the truth. She wasn't about to tell Gus what she really thought. He would hardly have been regarded as a sympathetic ally by his son over the issue of closing down those mines. But pointing that fact out to Gus now would serve no useful purpose.

"I have to go now, Caroline. I—I have to find Charlie so we can get up to that damned mine and find out what's going on."

"I'm on my way, too," she said calmly, calling on every last ounce of self-control she possessed.

"Do you know how to find Austin's cabin?" he thought to ask.

"Yes, I do."

"Follow the dirt road on past the cabin another mile or two. You'll see a turnoff on the right-hand side of the road. It's about another half mile or so up that track." Then Gus's voice cracked. "I pray that my son is all right."

It was then that Caroline's control began to snap. "I pray to God that *both* ours sons are all right...."

"Yes, of course. Of course," he repeated vaguely.

"Thank you for calling me, Gus. I'm leaving right now. I'll see you up at the mine." Caroline hung up the receiver.

But then she sat there for a moment, staring at the telephone. She swallowed the hysteria rising in her throat. She had to stay calm. She *must* stay calm. She had no choice now. There was no one to help her but herself. Her parents were in Colorado Springs. There was no time to try to reach them. This time she had to do it alone.

But, oh, dear God, what if Jeremy and Austin were lying in that mine shaft buried under a ton of fallen rock, the very essence of life slowly slipping away from them and no one there to help, no one there to give them comfort?

"Stop it, Caroline!" she cried aloud.

That kind of thinking didn't help. It was a waste of precious energy and even more precious time. The only thing that mattered now was what *was*, not what might be. And she wouldn't know that until she got into her car and drove up to the mine.

As she went to find her handbag and car keys, she couldn't help but remember the time when Jeremy was only three years old and he'd come racing around the corner of her parents' house. He'd run right into the side of it, banging his head against the hard wood. A huge goose egg had begun to form almost immediately on his forehead. He'd cried for a minute or two—perhaps startled more than actually hurt. She had called the doctor, of course, and followed his instructions to the letter, watching for any signs of concussion. When it was apparent later that afternoon that Jeremy was going to be all right, Caroline had sneaked off to the bathroom, turned on the cold-water faucet full force and cried her eyes out.

She would do the same now, she told herself as she got into her station wagon and backed down the driveway. She would save her tears for later.

But what if there was no later? What if she should lose her Jeremy now? Dear Lord, why of all nights hadn't she tucked him into bed last night? And why hadn't she got up this morning to say goodbye, to steal a kiss, as a mother often had to, while no one was looking?

And then another thought occurred to her. What if Austin should perish in that deep, dark mine and never know that she loved him? How could she live the rest of her life knowing she had never told him, never said the three simple words he had wanted to hear from her? How could she possibly carry that kind of burden with her until her own dying day?

She had to pull herself together. She was getting more morbid by the minute. A long list of "what ifs" never helped anyone; she knew that better than most. But she still prayed every mile of the way from her home to that mine high in the Colorado Rockies.

THE REALLY FRIGHTENING THING, she recognized much, much later, was that she remembered almost nothing of that two-and-a-half hour drive into the mountains. When she arrived at the site of the cave-in, there were men and equipment and vehicles everywhere. She parked her station wagon between a police car, its red light flashing around and around on top like some kind of beacon, and a white emergency paramedic van.

Caroline got out of her car and walked up to the group of men nearest her. Once she had identified herself, they were sympathetic, but they seemed to have no additional information beyond the obvious fact that a specialized crew was working as quickly as possible to remove the rock and debris from the entrance to the mine. Someone offered her a cup of coffee, which she declined. And then it began—the waiting, the not knowing, the soul-wrenching minutes that stretched into one hour and then two and then into hours that seemed like days.

Somewhere along the way, Caroline found herself accepting a cup of lukewarm coffee in a Styrofoam cup, and a tasteless sandwich was pressed into her hands. It was the path of least resistance, after all.

Gus Perry arrived alone, his aging face drawn into even deeper lines of worry and concern. They stood together yet apart, each of them wrapped up in private thoughts, neither one knowing what to say to comfort the other.

It was some time later that afternoon when a young detective finally approached Caroline and drew her aside.

"What is it, officer?" she asked dazedly.

"Mrs. Douglas, we think we've apprehended the culprit," he said as he rubbed his hand along the back of his neck in a weary gesture.

His meaning didn't sink in for a minute. "You've apprehended the culprit?"

"Yes, ma'am. We found him in a pickup truck a short distance down the road from here."

It still didn't make any sense to her. "What do you mean you found him down the road? How do you know that this—this person is the one who did it, anyway?"

"When we found the guy, he was just sitting there in his pickup truck muttering to himself. As soon as he saw us coming, he confessed everything, Mrs. Douglas. He told us the whole story from beginning to end before we even had the chance to read him his rights." The detective shook his head. "Not that it would have made a whole lot of difference, I guess. The poor old codger doesn't seem to be in full possession of his faculties."

Caroline was starting to get the oddest feeling in the pit of her stomach. "Have you arrested this man?"

"Let's just say we have him in custody," the officer told her. "The situation seems to be a bit more delicate than we had first thought. The old man told us it was all a terrible mistake. He said he didn't mean to hurt anyone. He didn't even know Mr. Perry and your son were inside the mine shaft. He was only trying to scare Austin Perry."

Caroline knew what she had to ask next. She also knew the answer to her question before she voiced it. "Did the man tell you his name?"

The young detective nodded. "He says his name is Charles. Charles Perry. And that Austin Perry is his nephew."

"Uncle Charlie . . ." she murmured sadly, the pieces of the puzzle falling into place. It made sense in an awful, wasteful, tragic way. "Poor old Charlie, it's been so long since anyone took him seriously," she said to herself. Then she looked up at the man. "What have you done with him?"

"He was becoming irrational, ma'am. Guilt can do that in some cases. Apparently he was the one who set off the dynamite, then realized what he'd done and drove to a telephone and called the police before he came back here. By the time we found him, he was in pretty bad shape. The paramedics had to give him something to calm him down, and then one unit transported him off the mountain to the nearest medical center. They'll keep him there under close observation until this whole incident is straightened out." The officer looked over at the dejected form of Gus Perry. "I hate like hell to have to tell his brother what's happened, though."

Caroline drew a weary hand across her brow. "Perhaps you could wait a little while, then. Will it make any difference to the authorities if he's told now or in a few hours?"

"You've got a valid point there, Mrs. Douglas," he agreed, visibly relieved to have postponed, at least, that unpleasant part of his official duty.

"Thank you," she murmured, giving the man a half-hearted smile.

Suddenly a shout went up from the group of men clearing the entrance to the collapsed mine, and then another and yet another. Caroline turned and started toward them, her legs moving faster and faster until she was running the last few yards.

"What's happened?" she cried out to the first man she came to, her voice sharpened by fear.

"It looks like they finally cleared away enough of the debris to send somebody in," he told her. "A couple of guys are volunteering to be the first to go through."

Caroline moved as close to the mine entrance as they would allow her to. She stood with her arms wrapped tightly around her upper body as if this were the only way she could keep herself in one piece. She was vaguely aware of Gus's coming up to stand beside her, and she remembered reaching out to take his hand in hers.

She wasn't certain she was still breathing, but she could feel her heartbeat like a great throbbing in her throat. Ice-blue ice water seemed to run through her veins. She hated this feeling of helplessness, but she stood her ground, her eyes fixed on the opening that had been chiseled through the pile of rock and debris. She watched the volunteer carefully make his way into the mine shaft until he was out of sight. Several minutes later the crowd waiting outside saw him emerge again. The volunteer straightened up and looked back toward the opening.

Caroline's heart stopped. There was the shadow of another form behind him. Surely it was too small and too slender for a man. And then another figure emerged from the mine. This one was tall and broad shouldered, and even partially concealed though he was in the dark shadows cast by the majestic fir trees overhead, she knew who it was! She knew!

At that moment she heard the sweetest sounds she could ever hope to hear if she lived a thousand lifetimes. One familiar voice called out to her; a second quickly followed.

"Mom!"

"Caroline!"

She began to run toward them, their names forming on her lips, but no sound would come from her mouth. Her heart and her mind were shouting their names with joy. Surely they could hear—surely they could hear her happiness!

And then a pair of thin arms threw themselves around her, and a soft, curly head was buried in her breast. Caroline held her son to her in a way she had held him only once before, in those precious moments at his birth.

As if that weren't enough for one woman in one lifetime, another pair of arms went around her, strong arms that held her, strong arms that gave her strength just when she needed it most, that trembled with the sheer joy of holding her. Even as she drew Jeremy closer, Caroline lifted her face and gazed up into the ocean of blue that was Austin Perry's eyes.

They heard a roar that swelled into one loud, rousing cheer from the dozens of rescue workers standing all around them. Joyous confusion reigned for the next few minutes as Austin reluctantly released her to go to his father, and Jeremy stood there, a little tired, a little thirsty and more than a little hungry, but apparently none the worse for his experience.

"I wasn't really scared, Mom," he told her as he wolfed down one stale sandwich after another that a member of the crew had brought him. "After all, Austin was there. He knows that mine like the back of his hand. He would have found another way out if he'd had to. I knew he wouldn't let anything happen to us." He looked up at her then with the unequaled confidence of youth. "You weren't really worried about us, were you, Mom?"

She blinked several times in quick succession and gave him a watery smile. "A little. Maybe just a little, darling."

"We were worried about you, too," came the husky voice of Austin Perry from behind her.

Caroline turned and walked straight into the man's waiting arms. She couldn't speak for several minutes, and she didn't want to. She just wanted to stay where she was for the rest of her life.

Finally she raised her head, looked up at him and whispered for his ears only, "If you had died in that infernal mine, Austin Perry, I would never have forgiven you." She tried to swallow the tears that threatened to overcome her.

"I would never have forgiven myself," he said with a touch of his usual sardonic wit.

She went up on her tiptoes for a moment and brought her mouth to within a fraction of an inch of his. "There's something I've been meaning to tell you." She could feel the precious breath of his life mingling with her own and the sweet touch of his tongue as he caught a salty tear that strayed down her cheek.

"What have you been meaning to tell me?" he repeated, knowing in that instant that simply the sound of her voice would always be enough for him.

Caroline decided to place her fate in his hands. She put her head back and stared up into his eyes, hiding nothing from him, keeping nothing back as she whispered, "I love you, Austin Perry. I love you with all my heart."

He seemed stunned. Then the import of her admission hit him, and his mouth came down on hers in a crushing kiss that ended much, much too soon for both of them. "You picked one hell of a time to tell me!" He swore softly as he drew back.

She gave him a tremulous, almost apologetic smile. "But better late than never?"

"Always," he assured her, dropping one last, quick kiss on her mouth as if that were as far as he could trust himself right now. Suddenly he was deadly serious. "Look, there's still some official business I have to take care of with the police."

Caroline lowered her voice again. "I know. It's about poor Uncle Charlie, isn't it?"

His eyes narrowed. "He could have killed us."

"But he didn't," she reminded him. "And he never meant to."

"I know." Austin sighed, looking very tired. "The worst part of it now is going to be telling Gus," he admitted as he glanced over his shoulder at his father. Gazing back down into Caroline's face, he added, "I'll get back to you as soon as I can. I just don't know when that will be. Will you be waiting for me?"

"I'll be waiting for you," she vowed.

Austin turned to Jeremy then and brought him into the circle of his embrace. The three of them stood there together for a moment before Austin said, "You two take good care of each other until I get back."

"We will," they promised as Austin released them. He turned and walked toward the older man and the police detective who were waiting for him.

Caroline and Jeremy gathered Jeremy's belongings and climbed into the station wagon for the drive back to Denver. They stopped at a local pizza parlor and picked up a large pepperoni with extra cheese. It was Jeremy's favorite.

Her son managed to consume his usual quota of four pieces, Caroline noticed, while she found herself barely able to get one down. And that night Jeremy fell sound asleep right after his favorite television show.

It was Caroline who cried herself to sleep with two names on her lips and two names in her heart....

11

SHE KNEW THE EXACT MOMENT he pulled into her driveway the next evening. It was twenty minutes past eight.

Before Austin even had a chance to ring the doorbell, Caroline had the front door open. They stood there for a minute or two, simply staring at each other through the screen.

He seemed as tall as ever, she thought, but thinner. His face had an almost haggard appearance, and there were faint shadows under his eyes.

"You look exhausted," she said in a quiet voice.

Austin laughed tiredly. "I am."

She unlatched the screen door and pushed it open. "You better come in and sit down before you fall down."

"I must look even worse than I feel," he said with a mild attempt at humor.

He stepped inside, and Caroline closed the door after him. He followed her into the living room. They sat down on the big overstuffed sofa, and Austin leaned his head back against the cushions. He let his eyes close for a moment.

Caroline's heart contracted. "Did you get any sleep at all last night?"

"A few hours," he told her without opening his eyes.

She reached out and placed a comforting hand on his shoulder. "You shouldn't have come over tonight. You could have waited until tomorrow."

Austin opened his eyes, straightened and looked over at her. "I couldn't wait another day. I had to see if you and Jeremy were all right."

At the mention of her son's name, Caroline laughed lightly. "Jeremy is fine. In fact, he's staying at a friend's house tonight. One of the boys is having a whole gang over for a cookout, and Jeremy will no doubt keep them up half the night relating the story of his great adventure for the umpteenth time. He's become something of a celebrity among the neighborhood kids, and you have been elevated to the status of a hero, right up there with Superman and all the rest."

Austin smiled for an instant. Then he said in a quiet and determined voice, "Thank God he's all right. I would never have forgiven myself if anything had happened to him. As it is, I was a fool. I should never have ignored those warning letters, however harmless they may have seemed at the time."

She gave his shoulder a sympathetic squeeze. "You mustn't blame yourself," she said, and added more firmly, "I won't have you blaming yourself, Austin. You can't be held responsible for what Uncle Charlie did. How is he taking all of this?"

He sighed wearily. "He's racked with guilt and remorse, of course. He really didn't mean for the accident to happen the way it did."

"I know," she said quietly.

"Apparently, he got it into his head to frighten me by dynamiting that mine shaft while I was in the area and making it look like an act of God. I guess he figured I'd take it as some kind of sign and change my mind about closing down the other mines." He stared intently into Caroline's eyes. "I don't believe it ever occurred to Charlie that Jeremy and I might get caught inside. Now he's afraid we'll never forgive him."

"I've already forgiven him," Caroline said.

"So have I. I guess the question is, can Charlie forgive himself?" Austin said in a low, earnest voice.

"What will happen to him now?"

"For the time being, he's in the hospital under psychiatric observation. We won't press charges even if they decide he's mentally competent. After all, he is family. Gus is talking about the two of them taking an extended vacation. I think they may finally make that trip to California."

At the mention of Gus's name, Caroline became concerned again. "How did your father take it when you told him about Charlie?"

Austin's eyes darkened. "He took it real hard at first. He felt he was as much to blame for what happened as Charlie. I'd mentioned to him that Jeremy and I were going panning up by the old mine shaft, and he told Charlie, of course. In his mind, if he hadn't made such a point of opposing the closing of the mines in the first place, his brother would never have tried to protect his interests. It looks like Uncle Charlie took his responsibilities as the older brother even more seriously than any of us guessed."

"Poor old Charlie," Caroline murmured. "When you think about it, he's never really had anyone but Gus to look after. No wife. No children. No grandchildren. Just his twin brother."

"A hell of a way for a man to end up in the final years of his life," Austin muttered with great feeling. He reached out and took her hand in his. "I don't want to end up like that, Caroline, with no one to care for, with no one to love."

Her heart went out to him. "Surely you won't."

"I won't if you meant what you said to me yesterday." His voice grew softer. "Did you mean what you said?"

She nodded. "I meant what I said."

He seemed unable to speak for a minute. Then, "I know I've said some unkind, hurtful things to you in the past couple of weeks. I don't know what to say now to make it up to you except that I'm sorry. I am sorry, Caroline. So damned sorry. You'll never know how—"

She raised a finger to his lips. "Shh, darling, it's all right. I said some unkind, hurtful things to you, as well. Can't we forgive each other and put it behind us now?"

"Can you forgive me and forget?"

"Of course I can." She brought his hand to her mouth, turned it over and gently pressed her lips into the open palm. "Don't you understand even yet, Austin Perry? I love you."

There was a certain hesitancy in his manner. "I guess I'm half afraid to believe it," he admitted huskily.

"Well, don't be afraid. It happens to be true, and I'm not about to change my mind."

She could see he still wasn't totally convinced. "Just when did you change your mind?" he wanted to know.

Caroline took a deep, steadying breath. "After we argued on Saturday afternoon and you left the house, I had a little talk with Jeremy. He pointed a few things out to me that made a lot of sense. Sometimes children have a strange way of putting things into perspective, you know."

His blue eyes flickered with a hint of humor. "I don't know, but I can imagine."

"That night I started to really think about us for the first time, and about my feelings for you. I guess it was a case of not seeing the forest because of the trees. I knew I was attracted to you from the beginning, of course. But I tried to convince myself it was strictly physical."

"It was certainly physical," Austin agreed as he stretched his arm out along the back of the sofa and moved closer to her. His thigh was pressed against her leg, and, like a gentle breeze, his breath stirred the wisps of chestnut hair around her face.

Caroline tried to concentrate on what she was saying. Austin's nearness wasn't making it any easier. "Anyway, I tried to imagine my life without you...."

He put his hand under her chin and raised her face to his. "And could you?"

Suddenly it was all there in her eyes for him to see. He had only to look. "No," she admitted in a small voice, "I couldn't imagine spending the next moment without you, let alone the rest of my life." She took a quick breath and went on, the words tripping and falling over each other in their rush to be expressed. "I knew I loved you before the accident up at the mine, but I thought I had time, Austin, plenty of time to tell you, to show you. When I realized I might never see you again, never touch you again, never hold you in my arms and love you—" Her voice broke off. She swallowed her tears and finished. "Then I knew how precious every moment of every day can be. And I knew you were right. The only cage around me was the one I had put there myself."

His arms went around her then, and his voice was a mere rasp as he confessed, "You aren't the only one who's been doing a lot of thinking, Caroline. I had plenty of time for that when we were trapped inside that mine shaft. I was wrong to try to pressure you into marrying me when you weren't ready. I should have given you the time you needed." He raised his head and looked into her eyes. "And I should have said the words. I thought to show you, not tell you. I should have done both." His gaze brushed across her face as if every detail, however minute, was precious to him.

"I should have known from your touch, if not your words," she murmured, her voice quavering with emotion.

"But I want to say the words," he told her. "I need to say them." And he did. "I love you. I love you, Caroline Douglas. You are my first and my last chance to find the kind of love every man dreams of. With you I feel like I have found some long-missing part of myself. I didn't even know how much I missed you, how much I needed someone like you until I fell in love with you. You're so much more than I ever hoped for, than I ever thought I would have. I've waited for you all of my life. Finding you now only makes it that much sweeter, that much more precious to me. I know that wealth and power are nothing without love. They're less than nothing without you, Caroline."

She looked at him with the love in her heart growing stronger and stronger. "And I know, Austin Perry, that you will be my lover, my friend, my companion, for the rest of my life. Just when I'd decided that I didn't believe in heroes anymore, you came along, my sweet, sweet hero."

He gripped her hands in his until she was half afraid he would cut off her circulation. "I will devote myself to you. I will take care of you and protect you. I will try to be both strong and gentle."

That brought the tears to Caroline's eyes. Tears like sweet, gentle rain. "I know you will."

"I promise that I'll do everything in my power to be that man for you. To be that man for Jeremy."

"And I promise to try to be the kind of woman you want and need." A small smile flitted across her face. "The kind of woman you would have whittled out of wood for yourself."

"But you're very much a woman of flesh and blood, aren't you, my sweet Caroline?" he murmured as he reached for her again. "You're no woman of wood. You're all soft and warm and willing," he assured her as his hands found all those soft and warm and willing places through the layers of her clothing.

She breathed his name through her teeth. "Austin, love me. Make love to me now."

"But what about Edna and Harry?" He groaned in frustration as he found the inviting curve of her neck. "They could walk in on us at any time."

"No," she assured him. "My parents are in Colorado Springs until the end of the week. They thought I needed some time alone."

"I think *we* need some time alone," he countered as he undid the buttons down the front of her blouse and pushed it off her shoulders. Her lacy bra followed and his shirt, until they were bare chest to bare breast, hard muscle pressed to soft curves, crisp, teasing hair against silky skin. Austin stood up and offered her his hand. "Why don't you show me your etchings, Mrs. Douglas?"

Caroline accepted his hand and came up to stand beside him. "And where do I keep my etchings, Mr. Perry?" she murmured in a seductive voice.

"Why, in your bedroom, of course."

She led the way, and he was right behind her. There they quickly removed the rest of their clothing and stretched out side by side on her large walnut-burl bed.

"Love was slow to come to me, but it was worth the wait," she said as she went into his arms.

Then he kissed the very last of winter's chill from her heart, and she melted into him. He had saved her life once by coming into it. Surely he was saving her again by staying.

His kiss lighted here and there on her face, on her breast, and then lower still along her silky-smooth abdomen and the tender flesh of her inner leg . . . until she could feel that most intimate of kisses pressed between her thighs. His caress created a sweet, violent heat in her blood that threatened to raise her temperature to the boiling point.

"Austin!" she cried out as she instinctively arched her body against the sweet promise of his.

Her nails raked his buttocks as she urged him closer. She reached for him and held his manhood captive in the palm of her hand. A tremor ran through his body. Her power over him was quick and frightening and primordial. Yet she would stand alone against the world to keep him from harm. He was the strongest man she had ever known, yet she wanted to protect him. He was the kindred spirit she had searched a lifetime for, and now that she had found him, they were both whole.

And then he came to her, joining his body and hers, surging into her, filling her completely and utterly and most joyfully.

Caroline could feel and taste and smell him on her skin, just as Austin must surely feel and taste and smell her on himself. The experience was seductive, erotic, provocative. There was a perfect symmetry, a natural beauty, to the way his body fit hers. The way their tongues met and moved in a sinuous dance. Her breast was made for his mouth, just as she was fashioned to take him, all of him, and rejoice in the taking. As the moment of climax caught them both in its sweeping wake, they held on tightly to each other. It was a long time before either moved or spoke.

Caroline curled up at his side afterward and murmured into his cooling flesh, "I love you, Austin. I love making love with you."

"And I love everything about you, from the little toe on your foot to the soft, lustrous strands of your hair," he reciprocated, keeping her close to him.

"Hmm...I've never been this happy, this content, in my whole life," she whispered, rubbing her chin along his shoulder. "My family will be ecstatic for us."

"I'm pretty ecstatic myself," Austin murmured as he stroked the smooth length of her body. He rolled her over onto his stomach and let her stretch out along the length of him.

"I have only one more request."

"Only one?" he teased.

"Only one to begin with," she corrected, propping her chin on her hands and gazing into his eyes. "Will you marry me?"

He was very still for an instant. Then he said, "I thought you'd never ask. And the answer is yes—to both of your requests," he added with pure pleasure as he ran his hands over her shoulders and down her back until her smooth bottom was cupped in his palms. She could feel her body's quickening response to his caresses and his own body's answer. As she melted for him, he grew ready for her.

Caroline looked down into his eyes again, and into his soul. "Somehow I feel like it's my birthday and Valentine's Day and Christmas all rolled into one."

Austin gazed at her with the light of pure love in his eyes. "You know what they say, darling . . . it's Christmas all year if you believe it in your heart."

And their gift to each other was the greatest gift a man and a woman can share, a true gift of the heart—the gift of love.

Harlequin Temptation

COMING NEXT MONTH

#137 PLAYING FOR KEEPS JoAnn Ross

Top tennis star Serena Lawrence was used to playing the game and winning. But it seemed she'd met her match in devastating Alex Bedare....
(Second book in a trilogy.)

#138 KINDRED SPIRITS Cindy Victor

Robin's reunion with her natural mother was a moving and joyful experience. But meeting Jay really made her heart take wing....

#139 ALMOST HEAVEN Elaine K. Stirling

After spending a day ballooning with virile, enigmatic Dr. Adam Torrie, Nicole was having trouble keeping her feet on the ground....

#140 AS TIME GOES BY
Vicki Lewis Thompson

Sarah and Cliff both remembered when a kiss was just a kiss. But now that ten years had gone by, the fundamental things applied....

Janet Dailey
Americana

Don't miss a single title from this great collection. The first eight titles have already been published. Complete and mail this coupon today to order books you may have missed.

Harlequin Reader Service

In U.S.A.	*In Canada*
901 Fuhrmann Blvd.	P.O. Box 2800
P.O. Box 1397	Postal Station A
Buffalo, N.Y. 14140	5170 Yonge Street
	Willowdale, Ont. M2N 6J3

Please send me the following titles from the Janet Dailey Americana Collection. I am enclosing a check or money order for $2.75 for each book ordered, plus 75¢ for postage and handling.

_____	ALABAMA	Dangerous Masquerade
_____	ALASKA	Northern Magic
_____	ARIZONA	Sonora Sundown
_____	ARKANSAS	Valley of the Vapours
_____	CALIFORNIA	Fire and Ice
_____	COLORADO	After the Storm
_____	CONNECTICUT	Difficult Decision
_____	DELAWARE	The Matchmakers

Number of titles checked @ $2.75 each = $_____

N.Y. RESIDENTS ADD
   APPROPRIATE SALES TAX $_____

Postage and Handling $___.75___

                   TOTAL $_____

I enclose _____

(Please send check or money order. We cannot be responsible for cash sent through the mail.)

PLEASE PRINT

NAME _____

ADDRESS _____

CITY _____

STATE/PROV. _____